**Some comments on William Gerhardie and *Futility***

"I have talent, but he has genius."

—Evelyn Waugh

"To those of my generation he was the most important new novelist to appear in our young life. We were proud of his early and immediate success, like men who have spotted the right horse."

—Graham Greene

"A comic writer of genius."

—C. P. Snow

"Why was there no shouting about Gerhardie's *Futility*—shouting to reach the suburbs and the country towns? True, devastating. A wonderful book."

—H.G. Wells

"One of the funniest English writers of the century."   —Philip Toynbee

"It [*Futility*] is a living book. . . . it is warm. One can put it down and it goes on breathing."

—Katherine Mansfield

A REVIVED
MODERN
CLASSIC

FUTILITY

William Gerhardie in the family ballroom in St. Petersburg

# WILLIAM GERHARDIE

## FUTILITY

PREFACE BY EDITH WHARTON

A NEW DIRECTIONS BOOK

First published in 1922. Reissued as New Directions Paperbook 718 in 1991.
Manufactured in the United States of America
New Directions Books are printed on acid-free paper
Published simultaneously in Canada by Penguin Books Canada, Limited

**Library of Congress Cataloging-in-Publication Data**

Gerhardie, William Alexander, 1895-
    Futility / William Gerhardie.
            p.      cm. — (A Revived modern classic) (New Directions
    paperbook ; 718)
        "First published in 1922" — T.p. verso.
        ISBN 0-8112-1176-2
        1.  Soviet Union — History — 20th century — Fiction.     I.   Title.
    II.   Series.
    PR6013.E75F88    1991
    823'.912 — dc20                                                      91-16047
                                                                            CIP

New Directions Books are published for James Laughlin
by New Directions Publishing Corporation,
80 Eighth Avenue, New York 10011

# Contents

# PREFACE

THERE are few novelists nowadays, I suppose, who will not readily acknowledge that, in certain most intrinsic qualities of the art, the great Russians are what Henry James once called Balzac: the masters of us all.

To many readers of the western world, however, there was—there still is, despite the blinding glare which the Russian disaster has shed on the national character—a recurring sense of bewilderment in trying to trace the motives of the strange, seductive and incoherent people who live in the pages of Dostoevsky, Tolstoi, and their mighty group. In Balzac, at all times, the western mind feels at home: even when the presentment is obviously a caricature, one knows what is being caricatured. But there are moments —to me at least—in the greatest of Russian novels, and just as I feel the directing pressure of the novelist most strongly on my shoulder, when somehow I stumble, the path fades to a trail, the trail to a sand-heap, and hopelessly I perceive that the clue is gone, and that I no longer know which way the master is seeking to propel me, because his people are behaving as I never knew people to behave.

'Oh, no; we *know* they're like that, because he says so—but they're too different!' one groans.

And then, perhaps, for enlightenment, one turns to the western novelist, French or English or other, the avowed 'authority', who, especially since the war, has undertaken to translate the Russian soul in terms of our vernacular.

Well—I had more than once so turned . . . and had vainly hunted, through the familiar scenery of *vodka*, *moujik*, *eikon*, *izba*, and the rest, for the souls of wooden puppets who seemed to me differentiated only from similar wooden puppets by being called Alexander-son-of-Somebody, instead of Mr. Jones or M. Dupont.

Then I fell upon *Futility*. Someone said: 'It's another new novel about Russia'—and every one of my eager feelers curled up in a tight knot of refusal. But I had a railway journey to make, and the book in my bag—and I began it. And I remember nothing of the railway journey, of its dust, discomfort, heat and length, because, on the second or third page, I had met living intelligible people, Sons-and-daughters-of-Somebody, as Russian, I vow, as those of Dostoevsky or Goncharov, and yet conceivable by me because presented to me by a mind open at once to their skies and to mine. I read on, amused, moved, absorbed, till the tale and the journey ended together.

This, it seems to me, is the most striking quality of Mr. Gerhardie's book: that he has (even in this, his first venture) enough of the true novelist's 'objectivity' to focus the two so utterly alien races to whom he belongs almost equally, by birth and bringing-up—the English and Russian—to sympathize with both, and to depict them for us *as they see each other*, with the play of their mutual reactions illuminating and animating them all.

There are lots of other good things in the book; indeed, it is so surprisingly full of them that one wonders at the firmness of the hand which has held together all the fun, pathos and irony of the thronged sprawling tale, and guided it resolutely to an inevitable conclusion. 'It takes genius to make an end,' Nietzsche said; and, perhaps partly for that reason, the modern novelist seems often to have decided that it is the trifle more conveniently dispensed with.

Mr. Gerhardie's novel is extremely modern; but it has bulk and form, a recognizable orbit, and that promise of more to come which one always feels latent in the beginnings of the born novelist. For all these reasons—and most of all for the laughter, the tears, the strong beat of life in it—I should like to hand on my enjoyment of the book to as many other readers as possible.

EDITH WHARTON

# Part I
# THE THREE SISTERS

[The ' I ' of this book is not me.]

# I

AND then it struck me that the only thing to do was to fit all this into a book. It is the classic way of treating life. For my ineffectual return to Vladivostok is the effectual conclusion of my theme. And the harbour has been strangely, knowingly responsive. It has sounded the note of departure, and the tall stone houses of the port seem to brood as I walk below, and ' set the tone.' And because of this and the sense that I am marking time till the big steamer comes and bears me home to England I am eagerly retrospective...

When the *Simbirsk*, of the Russian Volunteer Fleet, had at last completely vanished, carrying away the three sisters to Shanghai, I came back to my room at the hotel. I had just moved in there. It was a bare and dingy room in a small and shabby hostel. A bed was eventually provided, but in lieu of bed-sheets I was to lie on a dirty table-cloth which was to serve again as table-cloth next morning when I had my breakfast.

' Is this sheet clean ? ' I asked.

' Yes,' said the boy-attendant.

' Quite clean ? '

' Quite.'

' Sure nobody slept on it ? '

' Nobody. Only the boss.'

Big drops like tears fell on the window-pane and instantly made room for others. A ruined writing-table stood in the corner. I sat down. I fingered a typically Russian pen with a no less typically Russian nib, such as one is likely to encounter in almost any Russian government department, and dipping it repeatedly into ink that was like syrup, I made a bold beginning.

When night came I lay there on the table-cloth, hungry and worried by enormous hungry bugs that bit like dogs,

and thought of Nina, Sonia, Vera, Nikolai Vasilievich and
his unconventional family. In the morning the rain
ceased.

I paced the country, now in the embrace of autumn. I
wandered in remote places by the sea, in the abandoned park
that used to be a park essentially for lovers, and thought of
them. Here the foliage was more dense, the corners more
secluded, the disorder more magnificent. I sat on an old
bench that had names and initials cut out with a pen-knife,
under the trees turning gold and auburn, and shivered in
the sharp autumn wind that sent the fallen yellow leaves
whirling down the alley. And the vast sea of Russian life
seemed to be closing over me.


## II


It was somewhat in the manner of an Ibsen drama with
retrospective revelations that I was initiated into the complicated affairs of the Bursanov family. I had been asked
to call by the three sisters, all speaking simultaneously—a
charming bouquet, the queen among whom I recognized
only too well, and I called on them one evening in mid-
summer at their *datcha*, at a seaside place ten versts from
Petersburg, a little bashful perhaps for I had not been
invited by their elders ; and I was met by the ' bouquet '
in the hall of the little wooden structure that hung out above
the sea. They sprang out to me successively, introducing
themselves in order of age.

' Sonia ! '
' Nina ! '
' Vera ! '

They were then sixteen, fifteen and fourteen. I think I
had told them that day when I had first spoken to them
that I could not for the life of me distinguish one from the
other, and had deliberately mixed up their names. It was,
of course, poor fun, but they, then almost children, had

seemed grateful for it and giggled, possibly for want of anything better.

I was led into a room full of people whose relationship I did not yet comprehend. By the presiding posture over the samovar I thought that I could recognize the mother, and I walked up to her, and she put me at my ease, talking Russian, I noticed, with an unmistakably German accent.

' You don't any of you resemble your mother very much,' I told Nina afterwards.

' She is not our mother,' Nina said. ' She is—Fanny Ivanovna.'

I should not have thought that that youngish-looking, rather short but handsome man, well dressed but somewhat sluggish in his bearing, was their father, by the negligent, almost contemptuous manner in which his daughters treated him. But Nina called out ' Papa ! ' and he turned round, and then I saw that she had his eyes, those steel-grey eyes softened by a charming, disquieting, side-long look that was hers to give; and every now and then she would look straight into your eyes—anybody's eyes—down into your very soul, bathing her soul in your soul, causing you to feel as though you were indeed ' the only man who really mattered in the world.'

And Fanny Ivanovna pestered the life out of Nikolai Vasilievich (that was their father) by always asking silly questions, and Nikolai Vasilievich would look bored and sullen and would wave his hand at her as if she were a pestering fly and say :

' Drop it ! '

Or he would imitate in an unkindly manner the pre-posterous way in which Fanny Ivanovna talked Russian. ' *Elektrichno !* How often have I told you that it's *elektrichestvo* ? '

' It's all the same,' said she.

Then the three sisters insisted on dancing the one-step and the hesitation-waltz, at that time just coming into vogue abroad, while Nikolai Vasilievich was ordered to play some wretched tune on the piano over and over again. And I thought to myself : What a bouquet !

The ravishing experiment over, it was suggested at dinner that we should all go to the local theatre to see Chehov's *Three Sisters*.

' Very well,' said Fanny Ivanovna, ' but Nikolai Vasilievich must come with us. That is the condition.'

Nikolai Vasilievich frowned.

' You'll be too many in the box as it is.'

' We can take two boxes,' I suggested.

' There is no excuse, Nikolai,' cried Fanny Ivanovna. And a dark shadow flitted across the handsome face of Nikolai Vasilievich. But still I did not understand.

It was not till the end of the second act of the *Three Sisters* that I had an inkling, my first intuition, that all was not well with the Bursanov family.

You know the manner of Chehov's writing. You know the people in his plays. It seems as though they had all been born on the line of demarcation between comedy and tragedy—in a kind of No Man's Land. Fanny Ivanovna and the three sisters watched the play with intense interest, as if the *Three Sisters* were indeed their own particular tragedy. I sat behind Nina, and watched with that stupid scepticism that comes from too much happiness. To me, buoyant and impatient, the people in the play appeared preposterous. They annoyed me. They distressed me intensely. Their black melancholy, their incredible inefficiency, their paralysing inertia, crept over me. How different, I thought, were those three lovable creatures who sat in our box. How careless and free they were in their own happy home. The people in the play were hopeless.

' Good God ! ' I cried and grasped Nikolai Vasilievich by the arm as the curtain fell upon the second act. ' How can there be such people, Nikolai Vasilievich ? Think of it ! They can't do what they want. They can't get where they want. They don't even know what they want. They talk, talk, talk, and then go off and commit suicide or something.

It is a hysterical cry for greater efforts, for higher aims—
which to themselves, mind you, are vague and unintelligible
—and a perpetual standstill. It's like Faust in Gounod's
opera who takes the hand of Marguerite in prison and
cries, " We flee ! We flee ! " while making no visible effort
to quit the middle of the stage. Why can't people know
what they want in life and get it ? Why can't they, Nikolai
Vasilievich ? '

Nikolai Vasilievich sat still and silent and very sad. He
shook his head gravely and his face darkened.

' It is all very well,' he said slowly, ' to *talk*. Life is not
so simple. There are complications, so to speak, entangle-
ments. It cuts all ways, till—till you don't know where you
are. Yes, Andrei Andreiech...'

He sighed and paused before he spoke again.

' Chehov,' he said at last, ' is a great artist.'

I walked home with them to their *datcha* along the dark
and muddy road—it had been raining while we were in the
theatre—Nina clinging to my arm.

## III

It was on one of those long, happy evenings which it had
now become my custom to spend regularly at their large,
luxurious flat in the Mohovaya in St. Petersburg, that I was
further initiated into the domestic affairs of the Bursanov
family.

They had been sitting silently for a time. Nina seemed
sad ; Sonia and Vera sulky. It was twilight, but no one
had thought of switching on the light. No one would dance.
I played the piano for a while, and then stopped.

' What is the matter, Nina ? ' I asked.

She was silent, and then said in her childish open manner,
' Oh, Papa and Fanny Ivanovna.'

' What have they done ? '

' They are always quarrelling, always, always, always.'

I paused, hating to appear intrusive.

' You know,' she said in that half humorous, half serious
way she had of speaking, and then paused a little, and then
decided to have it out. ' Papa and Fanny Ivanovna are not
. . . legally married.'

' I know,' I said.

' How did you know ? '

' I suspected it.'

' Did Vera tell you ? '

' I didn't ! ' cried Vera in loud protest. She was fourteen,
but tried to look two years older, and indeed succeeded.
' I'd never dream of telling such a thing.'

She was shocked and angry at the unjust accusation so
provokingly flung at her. It had seemed to me for some
time past that there was no love wasted between Vera and
her two elder sisters. Vera was different.

' We can't stand this any longer,' said Sonia. ' I am sick
to death of their quarrelling. Day and night, day and night.
If they'd only stop at least when we have guests. But no,
they are worse than ever then.'

I could bear her out there—that is, if I were really classed
as a guest. For I was, rather, what Nikolai Vasilievich
called ' *svoy chelovek*,' one of the family, so to speak, and in
my presence Nikolai Vasilievich and Fanny Ivanovna certainly let themselves go. They were like cat and dog. There
was no mercy shown, no gallantry displayed. Nikolai
Vasilievich gibed at her, imitating her murderous Russian
with a malicious skill that set the room shrieking with
laughter. Fanny Ivanovna, her white face flushing in
patches of unwholesome pink, would writhe with pain, and,
having gathered her forces, give back as good as she got.
Nikolai Vasilievich would snatch out some isolated word
that she had mispronounced and, adding some pepper of
his own, would fling it into the audience of friends and
strangers that he had asked to dinner, and so pluck out the
sting at her expense.

' I'm sick of home,' Sonia said. ' I shall run away.'

'How can you run away?'

'I'll marry and run away.'

'No one will marry her,' said Vera from her perch in the far corner.

Nina sat mute, wearing her natural expression half serious, half ironic.

'What do they quarrel about?'

Nina looked up at Sonia. 'Shall I tell?'

'Of course.'

'Aha!' Vera cried maliciously. 'Aha!'

'You shut up!' said Sonia.

Nina looked vaguely at the window.

'Papa wants to marry again.'

The rustle of Fanny Ivanovna's approach was heralded through the air.

She appeared.

'Andrei Andreiech!' she cried. She always greeted me in this way, with acclamation. 'How d'you do!'

'How dark! Nina! Vera! Sonia! Why don't you light up the *elektrichno*!'

'How many times, Fanny Ivanovna,' said Sonia sternly, 'have I told you that it is not *elektrichno*, but *elektrichestvo*?'

'*Ach!* It's all the same.'

'It's not all the same, Fanny Ivanovna.'

'Andrei Andreiech! What news?'

'None, I am afraid, Fanny Ivanovna.'

'Has Nikolai Vasilievich come?'

'You know he never comes,' said Sonia, 'and yet you always keep supper waiting.'

'I'm tired of waiting for Papa,' Nina said petulantly, lying back on the sofa and swinging her pretty legs.

'He is later and later every day,' came from Vera's perch. 'Fanny Ivanovna, I'm hungry.'

Sonia was really angry. 'I would rather he didn't come at all, than just come to sleep here. Let him stay there, Fanny Ivanovna. Let him!'

' *Ach !* I think he might still come if we waited a little longer. Are you very hungry, Andrei Andreiech ? '

' Say yes ! Say yes ! ' cried the three sisters. I was amazed at this open display of hostility towards their own father, especially from Sonia. I understood the look in Fanny Ivanovna's eyes.

' No, Fanny Ivanovna,' I said, ' not at all.'

' Well, then we'll wait just a little longer. He *promised* to come.'

There was a ring at the bell.

' It's Nikolai Vasilievich ! ' cried Fanny Ivanovna.

But Nina shook her head. ' Papa never rings so timidly. It must be Pàvel Pàvlovich.'

The three sisters sprang off their perches and dashed into the hall.

' Ah ! ' we heard Sonia's voice.

' Who is it ?... Kniaz ? ' shouted Fanny Ivanovna.

' No,' came the answer, ' the other one.'

' Oh, the Baron. They are both Pàvel Pàvlovichi,' sighed Fanny Ivanovna as though the fact distressed her ; but it was really because she disapproved of them both that she sighed.

Baron Wunderhausen, as barons do in Russia, came from the Baltic Provinces, spoke Russian and German equally well, excelled in French, knew English, was polite, cunning and adaptable to any circumstances, had big calf's eyes, was habitually somewhat over-dressed, twenty-five years of age, and had a billet in the Ministry for Foreign Affairs. He came regularly every evening, made love with his eyes, and we danced...

We danced, and then had supper, having given Nikolai Vasilievich up as we gave him up regularly every evening after waiting for him for two hours. His absence annoyed everybody, for they suspected where he was.

' I am going away,' said Nina as she danced with me.

' Going away ? Where ? '

' To Moscow,' she said, looking up. She had a wonderful

way of looking up at you when she danced. She had a charming way of speaking quietly, enigmatically, half humorously, half lovingly.

' For always ? ' I cried in dismay.

In answer she held up two fingers behind my head which was supposed to give me the appearance of a horned devil, and laughed. I revelled in her laughter.

' For how long ? ' I asked.

' Two months.'

' Why ? '

' To see Mama.'

' I didn't know you had a Mama in Moscow.'

' I have,' she made the obvious answer and I smiled, and she laughed and again held up the devil's horns.

' What is she doing in Moscow ? ' I asked, and felt it was a somewhat silly question.

' Living,' she replied. And it seemed to me that she blushed. And for some reason that blush seemed to tell me that there, too, there was trouble.

' Who are you going with ? '

' Vera. She is going back for good. Mama wants to keep her.'

' Aren't you sorry ? '

' No.'

' Good God ! '

' I am sorry to leave Sonia.'

' But you are coming back to her ? ' I asked anxiously.

' Yes, but I am sorry to leave her, all the same. I am sorry to leave Fanny Ivanovna,' she added.

' And Papa ? '

She reflected a little. ' No,' she whispered.

' And whom else ? ' I persisted, smiling into her eyes and trying to press my own claims.

' I won't tell,' she said.

' When are you going ? '

' To-morrow morning. We only decided last night, Fanny Ivanovna and I,' she said quietly, ' that I should go.'

' To take Vera to Moscow ? '

She smiled enigmatically. We danced two rounds before she answered.

' That's what we tell Papa."

I looked at Sonia, as she passed us with her partner, ' hesitating ' marvellously. She made a *moue* at me and smiled. I knew that she was happy. The Baron danced with that characteristic air of his which conveyed that it gave him pleasure to give pleasure.


IV


I saw them off next morning in the desolating atmosphere of the Nicholas Station on a cold November morning. They were wrapped in heavy furs. The men had turned up the collars of their *shubas* against the biting frost. There was snow on the platform. We walked up and down quickly in order to warm our feet. Nikolai Vasilievich presented a pitiable sight with his pince-nez all blinded with snow, his moustache frozen, and his nose, reddened by the cold, protruding from his turned-up collar.

' Nina,' he said.

' Yes ? ' She turned round.

' Don't go.'

' I must.'

' You won't come back. She will keep you.'

She shook her head.

' Don't go, Nina.'

' Don't go,' I said.

She stood thoughtful, in indecision.

' Don't, Nina,' cut in Nikolai Vasilievich.

She did not answer.

' Nina,' he said again.

' No, she must,' intervened Fanny Ivanovna. ' This is all nonsense ! She will go and come back quickly. Won't you, Nina ? '

' Yes,' said Nina.

She turned to me and slipped her hand under my arm. ' I won't let you go,' she said petulantly. ' You'll have to come with me.'

' You know I can't.'

' I won't let you go.'

' Nina,' I said.

' Yes ? '

' Come here.'

I took her aside.

' Nina, will you marry me ? '

She looked flippant and humorous and yet there was just a trace of seriousness in her look.

' Yes.'

I felt relieved—oddly as I might feel if I had just concluded a satisfactory business transaction.

The second whistle went, and with the other passengers they boarded the train. Nikolai Vasilievich came up to her to say good-bye and probably thought he might chance it once again.

' Don't go, Nina. Nina ! '

' I shall come back,' said Nina.

Then they all said good-bye to Vera, and no excess of emotion was displayed on either side.

' Good-bye ! ' was said again. Then the train moved, and they waved handkerchiefs.

V

I called on them one evening in Nina's absence and chanced to find Fanny Ivanovna alone. Nikolai Vasilievich, as ever, was out. Sonia had gone to see a friend.

' Sit down, Andrei Andreiech,' she said. ' I am always doing needlework, as you see...'

I took a chair.

' I do it.—It is extraordinary, Andrei Andreiech. I

thought I would do it so as not to think, but it's just the very work to make you think. And so I gave it up and began reading in order to forget, in order not to think, and I found, Andrei Andreiech, that I could not read because I *had* to think. I think all day and night. *Ach !* Andrei Andreiech.'

And I knew that she was going to confide in me.

' *Ach !* Andrei Andreiech ! Andrei Andreiech ! If you only knew.'

She glanced behind her at the door to make sure that nobody could hear her.

' *Ach !* Andrei Andreiech ! '

I waited patiently for her to begin.

She said ' *Ach !* Andrei Andreiech ! ' several times more and then began. She spoke in marks of exclamation.

' I suppose you know, Andrei Andreiech, that I am not Nikolai Vasilievich's——legal wife ? '

' I know,' I said.

' How did you know ? ' she turned on me.

' I suspected it.'

She paused.

' Well, now that you actually know so much, I feel that I must tell you everything, if only in fairness to myself. But don't tell the children. They would be shocked if they knew that I had told you.'

' No,' said I.

' *Ach !* Andrei Andreiech, you know... You know...'
She suddenly plunged into her native German, the foreign Russian tongue being inadequate to express her overflowing feelings, but now and then, quite unintentionally, she would employ some Russian word that came handy to her, that in her excitement she could not be bothered to translate as she proceeded to unload her feelings—an urgency too long deferred.

' Andrei Andreiech ! ' she said again and again in a kind of appeal to my sense of justice. ' *Sie sollen wissen* that I met Nikolai Vasilievich in Switzerland, in Basle, when he was

there on a cure, after he had separated from his wife. He
was very handsome. He is still very handsome, *ach* ! much
too handsome. You would not think that he was fifty-three.
——*Ach* ! Andrei Andreiech, I have so much, so very much
to tell you that I don't really know where to begin...

' Well, I met him. I knew that he was married ; he told
me so himself from the first. He was always straight and
honourable and above-board. He said that he had separated
finally from his wife and expected to get a divorce, and that
I was to come to Petersburg with him and wait till he got
his divorce, and then we were to be married at once. You
see, we loved each other.' She looked at me.

' Quite,' I said.

' I must tell you here,' she continued, ' more about myself
and my feelings and desires at that time. I belong (I hope
you will forgive me for saying it, but it is a salient point in
my tragedy) to a very proud family indeed. My father and
all my brothers were officers in the German Guards. Soon
after my father's death we lost all our money. I had to set
out in search of a livelihood because I, as the eldest sister,
had to ensure that my sisters' education was not interrupted
and that it should be possible for my brothers to remain in
the army. I had a good voice and...I went on the stage, into
musical comedy. And, Andrei Andreiech, curious, is it not,
that in spite of the fact that I and I alone kept the whole of
our family—my sisters, my brothers, my aged mother, my
grandfather, my grandmother and two of my aunts—they
were ashamed of me. You see, I became almost what you
would call " a star." I don't want you to misunderstand me.
I shouldn't have said that they were ashamed of me. That is
misleading. They were ashamed of my profession, as I
was myself, of course. I understood them. I revelled in my
sacrifice. I was young, good-looking then. Don't look at
me now, Andrei Andreiech. I have changed through
suffering and age. Then, suddenly, I was seized by a craving
for decency, respectability. You see, no woman really knows
what it means to be respectable until she's had to give it

up. I thought : if only I could marry a man who was
respectable and rich, who would be willing to support my
family ! My heart craved for the title, the status, of a married
woman because that title was denied me.

'And then came Nikolai Vasilievich.

'I loved him. Love was thrown into the bargain. It was
unexpected, irrelevant. And then love became salient,
supreme, altogether dominating ; and as I realized how I
loved him, so I realized that my family, my sacrifice and all
that this had once meant to me, were but of secondary importance in the face of my love. Love was some greater
thing—altogether greater. And Nikolai was rich. He owned
a large house in Petersburg and had gold-mining concessions
in Siberia. But that seemed a minor point. He was to get
his divorce and then we would be married.

'We came to Petersburg and immediately got busy with
the divorce. He visited lawyers. His friends and relatives
all intervened and gave him advice, some in favour of a
divorce and others against it. I did not at that time know
what a hopeless, cruel and heartbreaking thing a Russian
divorce really is. Nikolai's wife did all she possibly could
to prevent his getting a divorce. Eisenstein, the man she
ran away with before Nikolai Vasilievich and I met, had no
money. He was a Jew dentist, with no practice. They
succeeded in proving to Nikolai Vasilievich's satisfaction—
I never quite followed the case—that if he asked for a divorce
he would be compelled to plead guilty and so lose the
children ; and Nikolai Vasilievich was determined to keep
the children. On my advice, Andrei Andreiech. I had
begged of him, entreated him, insisted on it. " Divorce or
no divorce, you must keep the children, Nikolai," I said. I
knew that they would be spoilt, their lives marred and
wasted, if they fell into the clutches of their mother and that
Jew dentist. Yes, I insisted on it, Andrei Andreiech, even
if it meant that there was to be no divorce. And what that
cost me !

'For I hadn't told my people in Germany that Nikolai

was married at the time. I didn't want to add further injury
to their pride. I thought it would be a matter of a few weeks
and that then Nikolai and I would be married, and all would
be well. How could I know ? How could we know ?

' We had the children—and what sweet girls they were
—but no divorce. Nikolai sent money to his wife regularly
every month, so as to keep the children ; and so I lived with
him just as if I were his wife, and indeed few people knew
that I was not. We lived very happily. He sent money to
my large family in Germany, regularly every month, and
naturally they thought that I was married to him. How
could I tell them that I was not ? What did it matter after
all, provided that *they* didn't know ? I felt that it was my
duty to sacrifice my personal pride for Nikolai's children.
And such nice, tender, beautiful girls they were too, Sonia
and Nina, so loving, so good, so pretty, so obedient, so
well-behaved. Every one who saw them said to me :
" Fanny Ivanovna, what nice children you have. You must
be so proud of them ! " I was. And, Andrei Andreiech, I
didn't tell them, you know, that they were not my children.
It may have been wrong of me ; but I did not. I was really
so proud of them, Andrei Andreiech, and as I had sacrificed
the divorce for *them*...it made me feel as if they *were* my
own.

' Nikolai was still always sending money to his wife to
keep her quiet. She always threatened to make a nuisance
of herself. She wanted the money, too—badly indeed, because that man Eisenstein she lived with wasted her money
in speculation on the Stock Exchange. Often she would
demand money in excess, and when Nikolai refused, she
would come up to Petersburg, enter our house, or go to
their school and carry the children off to Moscow and keep
them there with Eisenstein. Once she even threatened to
bring a case against Nikolai Vasilievich on the ground that
he had run away from her *with me*, if you please ! She was
tired of Eisenstein, who had spent all her money and proved
a dismal failure in dentistry, and, I think, she was anxious

to get back to Nikolai. I was in the way, you see. So what
do you think she did ? She spread stories about me. She
said I was a German governess in her household and had
beguiled Nikolai into running away with me. She spread
this tale among our friends and relatives each time she came
up to Petersburg.'

'And what about the girls ? ' I asked. ' What did they
think of Moscow and their mother ? '

' Andrei Andreiech ! ' she pleaded with all the fervour of
a woman at a disadvantage. ' A mother is a mother to her
children, always, whatever she has been or is. She can plead
love and sympathy and unhappiness with success. But the
sudden changes certainly affected the children's characters.

' One evening on their return from Moscow, when we
had guests to dinner, Nina, who was only eight, said :

' " Do you know, Papa, Mama says that Fanny Ivanovna
is just a lap-dog you cuddle on your knee for a while and
then chase away."

' How that stabbed me . . . to the very heart !... But
Nikolai was kind to me. I looked after him. I worshipped
him. He would come to me in the evening and say :

' " Fanny, I don't know what I would do without you."
And then he would think of what he could say to comfort
me, and unconscious of my happiness (happiness, Andrei
Andreiech, because I trusted him implicitly) he would say :

' " When the children grow up we will get a divorce,
Fanny."

' " Never mind the divorce," I would say. " So long as
my people in Germany don't know, it is all I want. I am
happy, Nikolai, *really*. I know that I am your real wife. Let
the children grow up first. We must think first of the
children. Always, Nikolai."

' And then I would find myself returning to the question
of divorce involuntarily. You see, in my secret heart I
wanted his divorce so much. And I would say again :

' " We must not think of the divorce, Nikolai " ; just
to make him repeat his promise.

' " When the children grow up we will, Fanny. I will get a divorce then."

' And the children, as I say, were such a pride and consolation to me. There were moments when I looked at them and thought I wanted no divorce. Those were my best moments... when I thought that... that I did not really care whether he got it at all. Sonia and Nina were the compensation.'

' What about Vera ? ' I asked.

Fanny Ivanovna paused suddenly. She looked as if she were going to reveal an unspeakable secret, but then decided not to.

' Oh, Vera . . . she always lived with the mother. Nikolai Vasilievich hates her... She is different.'

There was another pause.

' We lived like that eleven years,' she said, and stopped.

' And now ? ' I asked, and was horrified at my disastrous question.

' And now,' she said, her face quivering with emotion, ' . . . he wants to marry . . . a young girl of . . . sixteen.' She burst into tears.

She sobbed hysterically, and I stood there, helpless, filled with pity and an eagerness to help, and not knowing how to do it—saying :

' Fanny Ivanovna . . . Fanny Ivanovna . . . don't cry...'

Then I tried to think of what was usually done on such occasions. I rushed for a glass of water.

When she had drunk it and wiped her tear-stained face with her little lace handkerchief, she continued, breathing heavily :

' He came to me one evening in April and said :

' " Fanny, I must talk to you very seriously."

' " And what might it be that you want to talk to me about so seriously, *du alter Schimmel* ? " I said, and followed him happily into his study, thinking that he wished to consult me about some business transaction. He often consulted me on his affairs.

' " Sit down, Fanny," he said, and I was astonished at his seriousness. I sat down and he seemed to be waiting till I was comfortably settled in my chair.

' " Fanny," he said, "—don't be frightened—I've got to marry Zina."

' Zina, Andrei Andreiech, was a girl in Sonia's school and Sonia's class, of Sonia's age. *Seventeen*, Andrei Andreiech.

' I laughed. I could see that he was joking. I thought of the date. It was April—not the first but the twenty-first—yes, I remember perfectly.

' " Don't laugh," he said. " I am perfectly serious. I must. I have thought of it all. I fought against it. I have thought of every possible way that I could settle it. There is no other way. I can't, Fanny. It is love, this time, *real* love. There is nothing that you can say that I have not thought of. There is nothing that you can say that will alter my decision..."

' " Nikolai ! You are mad ! *Du bist verrückt !* " I cried. " *Wahnsinnig !* "

' And again I tried to think that he was joking. But Nikolai is obstinate as a mule. Obstinacy runs in the family. His grandmother was like that. Nina has it from her father. Obstinacy ! What a terrible vice ! There is no reason, no meaning in obstinacy beyond further obstinacy. It's a disease. There is no strength, no character about it. The weakest thing on earth is so often obstinate. Take Nikolai. A weak and sloppy man, and such a mule ! ' She paused. ' Perhaps I like to think that it is obstinacy. I cannot bear, Andrei Andreiech, to think that it is love.

' " Nikolai ! " I cried, and laughed. I really felt it was funny. " Think of yourself ! Look at yourself in the glass. Romeo ! Look at your grey hairs and those wrinkles ! " (Those dear, dear wrinkles. He had acquired them in my time, and so I had an absurd conviction that they should be mine.) " You're fifty-three and she is a girl of sixteen."

' " *Seventeen*," he said, as though it mattered.

' " Seventeen ! " I cried. " Ha ! ha ! ha ! " I tried to
laugh, but it had no effect on him. I expect, too, that my
laughter lacked real merriment. " *O mein Gott! mein Gott!
mein Gott !* "

' " It is love," he said very seriously. " It has come late,
but still it has come at last, and I am proud—don't laugh—
I am proud that at my age I should be capable of such love.
I thought that I had loved, I *had* loved, *you*, Fanny ; but
this is the love that comes once only, to which you yield
gloriously, magnificently, or you are crushed and broken
and thrust aside. . ."

' " *Du bist verrückt, Nikolai*," I repeated. " *Wahnsinnig*. . ."
' And then I thought of my people. And then I cried. . .'
She fumbled for her handkerchief. She sobbed again.
Again I dashed for a glass of water, this time doing the job
gallantly, efficiently, as though I had been doing that sort
of thing all my life.

She was bent on going on.

' I cried and he cried with me and tried to console me,
but I only thought of what I could say to stop him from
taking this mad, disastrous step.

' He said, " I know it is terrible, heartbreaking for you,
Fanny, and the children. . ."

' The children, Andrei Andreiech—I had forgotten them !
I who had sacrificed everything for them, divorce and everything else, I had never given them a thought in my disaster.
I took it up, Andrei Andreiech, promptly—I even admit
somewhat dishonestly—for I was thinking more of myself,
of me. Me ! me ! me ! I had lived with him for eleven
years !

' " Think of your children," I cried. " Think of your
children, Nikolai. They are yours. They are not my
children, and yet I have sacrificed my life and my honour
for them."

' I tried to shame him, but I had to realize that indeed
nothing could shame him. I mean, he was already ashamed
to his full capacity, conscious of unpardonable sin, conscious

of being a bad man, the very worst man—had admitted it
all to himself. . . and was satisfied, as though this confession
to himself had cleansed him of his wickedness and he had
come out of it, clean, sanctified. That's what I couldn't
stand, Andrei Andreiech. That he should have told himself
that so good and wise and indeed well versed was he in his
own wickedness, that there could be no crime, no sin, of
which we others could accuse him of which he had not
already in his goodness and wisdom accused himself, and
so forgiven himself and started clear, afresh, with *our* lives
all wrecked and ruined—that's what I can't forgive him.
That's what Nina can't forgive him. But imagine our con-
sternation when he tells us that he had never really expected
our forgiveness when he had made up his mind to marry
Zina, his mind evidently having been made up in spite of
that knowledge. Why, it would be far better if he had not
realized how he had sinned than to plume himself on being
a sinner unavoidably and bowing to his fate so readily that
you almost suspected that, after the manner of his race, he
had bribed it heavily to please him. I am afraid I am over-
straining this point, Andrei Andreiech. But it is, after all,
*the* point.

   ' At last I sprang upon him. " What do you propose to
do, Nikolai ? What do you want *us* to do ? Speak, tell me ! "

   ' He shrugged his shoulders. " Live on as we have been
living, you looking after the children. What if I am married
to Zina ? I can still come home every night to you and the
children. It changes nothing."

   ' " *Nein, besten Dank !* " I said. " No, thank you, *blago-
daru vas !* I will return to Germany as soon as you give me
the money—provide for me for life. I will not leave
otherwise." '

   In her great tragedy she was still a sound business woman.

## VI

She was silent for some time.

'Andrei Andreiech, does she love him? Cannot live without him? "Don't you believe it," I told Nikolai Vasilievich. "She will leave you as soon as she has robbed you of your money."

'"Then I shall come back to you," he said.

'"Thank you'for nothing," I said. "I shan't want you then."

'Andrei Andreiech, it is all his money. It is really comic, but they all believe him to be preposterously rich. A house-owner in Petersburg! Gold-mines in Siberia! A million-aire! Zina's people keep telling her, "Stick to him, stick to him, don't let him go. These gold-mines in Siberia, these millions, this house in the Mohovaya!" That's all, in fact, they are after. Why won't his wife give him his divorce and be done with him? Because she believes in the gold-mines. Why does Baron Wunderhausen always hang about here? Why does he run after Nina, Vera and Sonia? The gold-mines again, and the house in the Mohovaya.'

'What of me!' I cried in horror. 'I come here every evening, Fanny Ivanovna, and stay till late in the night.'

'Oh, you are different.'

'I shall have to stop coming now.'

'You may as well dismiss at once from your mind any suspicion of an ulterior motive,' said Fanny Ivanovna, rising to the occasion. 'They are worth nothing, anyhow—both the gold-mines in Siberia and the house in the Mohovaya.'

'Worthless! You don't mean it?'

'Absolutely.'

'Do the gold-mines pay nothing?'

'Andrei Andreiech, I have lived with Nikolai Vasilievich now for over eleven years. I don't remember their ever paying a copeck. They may have paid before my time. But I doubt it. Nikolai Vasilievich, though, is constantly pouring money into them, every month, every year, to keep them going. And this, Andrei Andreiech, what with the money he has to fork out for his wife and Eisenstein and what we spend ourselves and what he gives Zina and her people, who are very poor, and '—she blushed—' what he sends my own people in Germany, and his own sisters and cousins and several other friends and dependants . . . why, Andrei Andreiech, it takes all he can scrape together...'

' But the house in the Mohovaya ? '

' Precisely. He has been compelled to mortgage the house to be able to manage at all . . . and keep the other thing going.'

I whistled under my breath. I remember how Baron Wunderhausen had grasped me by the arm one day as he spoke with enthusiasm of Nikolai Vasilievich.

' Rich as Crœsus,' he had said.

Well, I felt sorry for him.

I heard a little nervous cough and a rustle, and a harmless little old man, like a mouse, whom I had not noticed in the room before, rose and walked out.

I was horrified.

' Fanny Ivanovna,' I cried, ' that man has heard everything you've said.'

' Oh, *Kniaz* ! ' she said with undisguised contempt. ' He's heard it all before.'

I felt that this startling news rather took the gilt off the confession. I had flattered myself on being the first, in fact the only one.

' He's heard it many times,' said Fanny Ivanovna. ' Every now and then I feel that I absolutely must confess it all to *somebody* . . . no matter who it is.'

' I thought,' I said a little reproachfully, ' that you had told nobody, Fanny Ivanovna.'

' Andrei Andreiech ! ' she cried in her tone of appeal to my sense of justice, ' I haven't spoken of it to anyone for more than two weeks. If you hadn't come here to-day, I don't know. I really think I should have confessed it to the hall-porter. You don't understand.'

' I do understand,' I said, but I could not help feeling misused and mishandled. I almost begrudged her the gallantry of my dash for water—two separate dashes, to be exact—when I remembered that they must have been carried out by other men before me, the confession to-night being, of course, an exact replica of the confessions that had preceded it, Lord knows how many times, like a melodrama with its laughter and hysterics occurring always at the proper interval as it is produced each night. And I was led to revise my recently adopted theory that I was indeed a born confidant by virtue of my understanding personality, tempting strange women into thrilling, exhilarating confessions of their secrets. Rather did I feel the victim of a lengthy and tedious autobiography inflicted on me under false pretences.

I heard the sound of the outer door closing on the old Prince.

' Kniaz,' said Fanny Ivanovna, ' is also one of those who live on Nikolai Vasilievich. He always comes here. Never misses a day. Sits, reads, eats, and then goes. And all without uttering a word. When he borrows money from Nikolai Vasilievich he naturally opens his mouth, and then shuts it until the next occasion.'

The old Prince was one of those quiet nonentities who enter unasked and leave unhindered almost any Russian home ; and no one is likely to object to their coming because no one is likely to notice them. They have a face, a name, a manner so ordinary that you cannot remember them, ever. They are so colourless, so blank that they seem scarcely to exist at all. I think Goncharov speaks of them somewhere, but I would not be sure of it. ' Kniaz ' was like that. His name was some very ordinary name, and it even seemed odd that he should not have a more exclusive name for his title. But no one cared. No one, to be sure, knew what his name was. His *imya otchestvo* was Pàvel Pàvlovich, like the Baron's, and so he was called by all but Fanny Ivanovna, who called him ' Kniaz,' sarcastically—a Prince without a copeck to his title ! I only remember that he was always very neatly dressed, shaved regularly and wore a very stiff and sharp collar which seemed to torture his dry and skinny neck.

'Kniaz has some shares,' she explained, 'in a limited company, but they are worthless—always have been—and never paid any dividends. Never so long as anybody can remember.'

'Has he always lived on you, then ? '

'He lived on his brother when he was alive. He had great expectations from his brother. But his brother died and left him more shares, quite a number of shares, in the same limited company. Whom the brother lived on when he was alive, Lord only knows ! '

'Did they get their shares from their father ? '

'Their uncle.'

'Did *he* get any dividends ? '

'Nikolai says no. But he seems to have put all his money into them.'

'And now I suppose you invite Kniaz to come and live with you ? ' I asked.

'He comes of his own accord.'

'You don't object to his coming ? '

'No one would tell him even if they did. It's not a Russian habit to object to anyone who comes to your house. It isn't much good objecting either. They'll come anyhow. But never mind.'

'Extraordinary man. What does he propose to do ? Has he any plan ? '

'He believes in the shares.'

'Have you ever tried to disillusion him ? '

'I wouldn't be so heartless.'

'And the girls ? '

'For them money does not exist. They are sublimely indifferent to it.'

'And Nikolai Vasilievich ? '

'Nikolai Vasilievich believes in the mines. Kniaz helps him to sustain that belief in return for Nikolai's faith in the shares. The money Kniaz borrows from Nikolai Vasilievich he regards merely as an advance on his future dividends.'

' And does Nikolai Vasilievich regard it in that light ? '

' He pretends he does. But he always says : " Never mind, if only the mines begin to pay all will be well, Pàvel Pàvlovich." '

' And the " family," Fanny Ivanovna,' I cried, ' I mean his wife and her family, his fiancée and her family, you and your family, his sisters and cousins, Kniaz and the others and their families—do *they* believe in the mines ? '

' More firmly than Nikolai. If, in fact, one fine day Nikolai turned a sceptic in matters mining, they would, I am sure, suspect him of shamming poverty to prevent them from getting their legitimate share.'

' Fanny Ivanovna,' I sighed, ' good night.'

' I know it is amusing. I wish it wasn't real life, our life, my life. Then I would find it a trifle more amusing.'

I hailed a driver who slumbered in his sleigh on the corner of the Mohovaya and the Pantilemenskaya. As I drove home across the frozen river, on which the moon spread its yellow light, I thought of the Bursanovs' muddled life, and then Chehov's *Three Sisters* dawned upon my memory. I understood now why Nikolai Vasilievich sympathized so heartily with the people in the play.

## VII

That evening I remember as an ever-deepening initiation into the very complicated affairs of the Bursanov family. It had been raining again, and the washed cobbles on either side of the street looked clean and shining as if newly polished. For once Nikolai Vasilievich was at home, but he had gone into his study, and, sitting at the piano, I could not help listening to what was said in the room.

' But Mama *does* want a divorce herself, Fanny Ivanovna,' —from Nina.

' She didn't before,' said Fanny Ivanovna.

' She does now,' said Nina.

' I wonder why ? '

' I don't really think, Fanny Ivanovna, that you have any right to know that.'

' She can't have a divorce, anyhow,' said Fanny Ivanovna. ' And I have asked you to make that clear to her.'

' You see,' said the girl of fifteen, ' Mama has her own point of view. She doesn't look at things from your point of view. Why should she ? '

' Why should she . . . ' repeated Fanny Ivanovna. And there was a long pause.

' I've done what you asked me,' said her ambassador, shrugging her pretty shoulders.

I stopped playing.

Nikolai Vasilievich came back and we sat down to dinner, and amongst us appeared Vera. I was to understand her presence a little afterwards. The atmosphere was tense. No doubt they had all been discussing the family tangle. No doubt Nikolai Vasilievich and Fanny Ivanovna had been shouting and blackguarding each other as usual. But silence reigned for the moment. It was as if they had all been a little overstrained by this uncanny family burden. Then there was a ring at the bell.

It was merely the postman, and the maid brought in a letter for Fanny Ivanovna. So soon as she caught sight of the envelope she got flushed and wildly excited.

' It's from Germany,' she cried, and something about her flush, about her manner, told us that the letter was a painful reminder of her painful circumstances, rather than a joy. She tore it open, and for some reason the room grew still : all seemed to watch her in perfect silence. And then she fluttered the letter and flushed again, and cried out to Nikolai Vasilievich in a voice of deep sorrow and reproach, as a tear welled up from her eye :

' Listen.—" Dear Fanny—*and Nikolai !* " *And Nikolai ! And Nikolai !*—Do you hear : *And Nikolai !*—'

'Nikolai—i—i—' echoed with pathetic insistence. It was a sound that rent the heart. Tears flushed her eyes, sobs choked her throat. And for the moment, at all events, they forgot her clumsy stupidities ; they felt only how irreparably they had wronged her.

And then, like the announcement of the next act, there was another ring. We heard an unfamiliar voice inquire in the hall if Nikolai Vasilievich was at home. Then the visitor's card was brought in by the maid.

'No !' said Nikolai Vasilievich, rising very emphatically. 'I draw the line there.' And he walked away to his study.

Fanny Ivanovna, her tragedy forgotten in the excitement of the visit, snatched at the card.

'Eisenstein !' she exclaimed.

'*Och !*' cried the three sisters in disgust.

And then, uninvited, unannounced, Eisenstein walked into the dining-room.

He was a tall, flabby man, with prominently Jewish features, and probably good-looking as Jews of that type go.

'Nina,' he said, looking round. 'I want to see Nina. I missed seeing her in Moscow.'

'Yes ?' Nina said, 'I am here.'

Fanny Ivanovna looked at Eisenstein with scrutiny. I think she could feel no real enmity to this man because he had, after all, run away with Nikolai Vasilievich's wife—to all appearance a necessary preliminary to her own advent into his life. It was quite obvious that Eisenstein was not in the least seeking a *tête-à-tête* with Nina, but on the contrary, desired to exhibit his overflowing emotions to as large an audience as possible.

'Nina,' he said, halting in the middle of the room. And I remembered that Eisenstein had been an actor in his youth, a conjurer and ventriloquist. 'Nina, she mustn't leave me. You who have such influence over your mother must insist on that.' And sooner than anyone had been prepared for it his body quivered and he wept bitter tears.

' Moesei Moeseiech,' Nina said, ' you mustn't cry. That won't do at all.'

' Monsieur Eisenstein,' intervened Fanny Ivanovna, rising dramatically, ' this is my house and I won't allow it.'

' You leave him alone, Fanny Ivanovna,' said Nina.

' I can't bear it, Nina,' he said, coming up to her. ' Why must she leave me ? Haven't I always been very kind to her, Nina ? She says I speculate. But why do I speculate ? For *her*, Nina.'

' For her ! ' cried Nina in bewilderment.

But he misunderstood her intonation.

' Why, of course ! '

' With her money, Moesei Moeseiech ? '

' My dear child, even if it is her money, what of it ? I am still doing it for her, trying to get her more. My heart bleeds for her. She has so little money. Your father in his immoral pursuits of other women has forgotten his own wife.'

' Moesei Moeseiech, leave us.'

' But why, Nina ? '

' You're . . . hopeless.'

' Hopeless ? And you say that, Nina. Haven't I always been a good father to you when you came to live with us at Moscow ? Haven't I always been a good father to you ? Now, have I not ? Nina, Nina ! You alone can stop her.'

' I've had too many fathers, Moesei Moeseiech, and I am not sure, if not too many mothers.' She paused. But when he opened his mouth to speak, she rose abruptly, turned on her heel and left the room.

Fanny Ivanovna rose a second time.

' Monsieur Eisenstein,' she said, ' you have upset everybody. I must ask you to leave my house. I cannot have you exhibiting your domestic difficulties in this strange manner before our friends. We all have our sorrows, but we must keep them to ourselves. They are of no interest to others. Please leave us.' Again she must have thought of him as the man who had delivered Nikolai Vasilievich from his wife. She had a kind look for him, but she was a determined lady.

But for not being put out even by the most determined lady, give me a Russian Jew. Eisenstein looked round and saw Vera in the twilight, mute and hostile, perched up on the armchair in the corner.

' Vera ! Vèrochka ! ' he cried. ' You, my daughter——'

' S—s—s—sh ! ' Fanny Ivanovna hissed like a serpent. ' You must not ! '

' Must not, why ? Why mustn't I ? ' he said with that characteristically Jewish intonation. ' Why should I be ashamed of my own daughter ? You treat me as if I was an outsider and didn't belong to the family. Why should my daughter be ashamed of me ? She *is* my daughter, and you know it, Fanny Ivanovna.'

Whether this was a revelation to Vera, or only a confirmation of what she already knew or had perhaps suspected, it was hard to tell. She sat there on her perch, mute, aloof.

' Now,' said Fanny Ivanovna, coming up to him with indomitable determination, ' you must certainly go.' And he left the room, sobbing.

' How horribly he cried,' said Sonia. I followed her out into the drawing-room. When I returned I perceived that Vera was wiping her tear-stained eyes and telling Fanny Ivanovna who had evidently been consoling her :

' And I had hated him so… Oh, I still hate him so . . . so…' She half sobbed again, wiping her tear-stained face with her little handkerchief. And I thought that I could now discover something Jewish about her pretty features.

And then there was another bell. It seemed that evening that it was one long succession of bells each carrying in its trail some fresh dramatic revelation, as though we had been privileged to witness some three-act soul-shattering melodrama. It was to be a night of bells and sobs.

## VIII

This time there was a good deal of whispering between the maid on the one hand, and Sonia and Nina and Vera on the other. Then the three sisters vanished into the hall, and there was more whispering. It seemed that the heavy front door had been only half shut and that they had all gone out on to the landing.

About five minutes later they returned to Fanny Ivanovna, purring round her like three pretty kittens, till Fanny Ivanovna became suspicious. Then they grew still, and a mysterious look came on Nina's face.

' Fanny Ivanovna,' she said.

' Yes ? '

'Will you do something for me, Fanny Ivanovna ? '

' I will. You know, Nina, that I will do anything for you, anything—reasonable.'

' I'm afraid you will think it unreasonable, Fanny Ivanovna.'

' What is it ? ' said Fanny Ivanovna, for some reason looking round at me, as though I were a party to the conspiracy.

Nina looked at Sonia, and Sonia nodded.

' Mama is outside—on the landing. She wants to see you. Will you see her ? Please, Fanny Ivanovna, *please.*'

I understood now why Vera had come back to Petersburg.

' *Please !* ' cried Sonia.

' *Please !* ' echoed Vera.

Fanny Ivanovna rose very swiftly, as if by the swiftness of her movement she intended to intercept at the root that which she considered quite inadmissible.

' No ! ' she said, colouring highly. ' No ! '

' Fanny Ivanovna, *please !* '

' No, Nina, no. It's out of the question.'

' Oh, Fanny Ivanovna, *please !* ' they entreated her. ' She is our mother, Fanny Ivanovna. We can't have our mother waiting on the landing. After all, she's our mother.'

' *After all*,' said Fanny Ivanovna, putting a terrible meaning of her own into these simple words, ' *after all*, I am the mistress of this house. True, I have been thrown into the mud and trampled on, told I am not wanted, done away with, about to be thrown into the street like a dog, but while I am here I am the mistress of this flat. *After all*, I am ! ' she cried out, almost in tears.

' Very well, then, I will never speak to you again,' said Nina.

The three sisters again vanished on the landing, and whispers were renewed, and Fanny Ivanovna resumed her needlework, her agile fingers, it seemed to me, moving quicker than was their custom.

' The lap-dog . . . ' she whispered, turning her face to me. ' The German governess . . . Andrei Andreiech, why should I ? Why should I ?. . .'

When at last the three sisters returned from the landing, such depressing silence descended upon the room that I thought I would do well to follow the example of the two Pàvel Pàvlovichi and go home. There was no one to see me out this time. As I reached the lower steps of the broad winding staircase I heard the faint sound of a woman weeping. Then I could see a dark silhouette between the large glass double-doors leading out into the dim street. It was also dim in the vestibule. As I came nearer I saw that it was Magda Nikolaevna Bursanova.

My first impulse was to dash upstairs for a glass of water. But the sobs died away at my approach.

It was still raining heavily.

I raised my hat.

' I have sent the porter for a cab,' she said, wiping her tears hurriedly. ' I don't know if he'll get one now. It's raining terribly.'

And as we waited, before I knew where I was, she too began her confession.

' You must have heard of me very often,' she said in her gentle, musical voice. She was a very gentle-mannered

woman and in her youth she must have been curiously like
Nina. She even had, I thought, the side-long look. ' I am
sure,' she said, ' I shouldn't like to hear all that you have, no
doubt, been told about me.'

Then she added :

' I know you. Nina has spoken of you. But there is one
thing, Andrei—I don't know your——'

' Andrei Andreiech.'

' There is one thing, Andrei Andreiech, that I want to
know. Why, why can't we put our heads together and
decide something, help each other, instead of standing on
our silly dignities ? Heaven knows that we are in a muddle.
Heaven knows that we have all of us sinned in our own small
way, Andrei Andreiech. I came. I wanted to see her, to
arrange things, to have it all out. I want to marry and leave
them. I want Nikolai to give me a divorce. Then I will
leave them alone. They can all do just as they please. I bear
no one any malice.

' I came, and I was not admitted... Into my own house,
my own flat. It was my flat, Andrei Andreiech. I chose it.
I bought the things and arranged them. There isn't a single
thing in here that wasn't mine. When all is said and done,
they are *my* children, Andrei Andreiech. And I have to wait
outside like some low hawker—a *tatarin*—on the landing
. . . not admitted...' She was about to sob again, but then
thought better of it and replaced her handkerchief.

' But, Andrei Andreiech, to send my own daughter to me
to Moscow as a kind of emissary to ask me on no account
to grant Nikolai Vasilievich a divorce, so that he should
be unable to marry again—I call that low, low... All this
time she has wanted a divorce—reproached me, in fact, for
standing in the way. What has it to do with me ? If Nikolai
really *wanted* a divorce, how could I have prevented him
from getting it ? '

' He would lose the children,' I explained.

' Why should he lose the children ? ' she asked.

' It's the Russian law.'

Magda Nikolaevna laughed. 'Are you a law student ? '

' No.'

' I thought not.'

' Why ? '

She laughed again. She had, I noticed, a very wicked laugh.

' Andrei Andreiech, you are very, very young, and believe everything you hear. If I am in the wrong and he is in the right, is it likely, I ask you, that under any conceivable law Nikolai should lose the children ? It is the one who is in the wrong that loses the children. If Nikolai does not want a divorce because he does not want to lose the children, he knows that he is in the wrong.'

' So you think that is the reason he doesn't want a divorce ? ' I said, and then added, ' Of course I knew that.'

' Ah, but you didn't know *why* he would lose the children by a divorce. If you are logical you must admit that it is so. It's either so, or——'

' Or ? '

' Or Nikolai simply did not want a divorce.'

' Why ? '

' Perhaps he didn't want it.' She shrugged her shoulders and laughed wickedly. ' You see, you can't have it both ways. Either he didn't want a divorce because he didn't want to lose the children, in which case he obviously admits that he is in the wrong. Or,' she laughed wickedly, ' he merely says so to Fanny Ivanovna, who is stupid and knows no better, because he does not want a divorce . . . so as not to marry her.'

' But he does want a divorce,' I said.

' *Now*,' said Magda Nikolaevna. ' I suppose you know why he wants it now ? '

I nodded, and she nodded in answer—I thought rather significantly. I remembered that it had always been her wish to read for the Bar, but her own life had been too busy and complicated by legal proceedings to admit of the leisure necessary for the pursuit of her hobby.

'You know only half the story, young man,' she said.
'You know, for instance, that I ran away with Eisenstein.
But you don't know *why* I ran away with Eisenstein.'

'I am sure I don't want to,' I said, 'if that is not being
very rude.'

'Half-truths are more dangerous than lies,' said she. Here
the porter returned with a cab.

She searched in her little bag for a coin, but I anticipated
her.

'But you must,' she said. And dragging me after her
under the raised hood of the cab and seated therein comfortably she was about to begin a long story, but suddenly
checked herself.

'It's rather absurd,' she said and then laughed softly,
which for the moment made her seem to me again curiously
like Nina, 'that I should be telling you why I ran away *with*
Eisenstein at a time when I ought to be telling you why I
have just run away *from* him.

'I am going to marry,' she said.

'Yes?'

'An Austrian, Cecedek. Do you know him?'

'No.'

'Andrei Andreiech,' she said suddenly, as we sat under
the dripping roof, bouncing softly over the cobble-stones,
'why don't you go in for law? It's so interesting.'

And glad of a change of subject I told her why I did not
propose to read law. But as we turned on to the Liteiny
and began ascending the convex bridge, she bent eagerly
towards me and told me in great detail why she had run
away with Eisenstein and why she was now running away
from him.

## IX

It was a day, I remember, of a peculiar warmth and fragrance, when you could feel that winter has become spring.
I was strolling down the Nevski, and upon the wide, lighted

splendour of this queen of streets I ran into Nikolai
Vasilievich, with a pretty flapper on his arm.
' Andrei Andreiech ! '
' Nikolai Vasilievich ! '
And we shook hands warmly.
' May I introduce——? '
And I was introduced.
I could hardly recognize him. His careworn look seemed
to have deserted him in his dissipation, as if ashamed to
accompany him thither. He seemed ten years younger in
her presence. He was smarter, bore himself better, seemed
actually taller, bigger... Oh, was it at all the same Nikolai
Vasilievich who wrangled so furiously with Fanny Ivanovna ? This Nikolai Vasilievich was as happy as a school-
boy. But before we had walked ten yards Nikolai Vasilievich
was already expatiating on his unhappy family affairs. ' Well,
well ! ' he sighed. He rather liked to sigh over his sins ;
indeed it appeared that his distressing family burdens formed
the sole subject of his conversation with this engaging
flapper.
' I keep telling Nikolai,' said Zina, ' " don't marry me,
don't. It is superfluous. I love you so much that I am
perfectly prepared to live with you . . . just to show you
how I really love you." What is marriage ? A piece of paper.
It's absurd. It means nothing. What do *we* care ? What do
I care ? I have been reading Verbitskaya's *Springs of Happiness.* She seems to agree with me.'
' No,' said her noble lover, ' I wouldn't think of taking
advantage of your innocence. Verbitskaya is a fool. It
would break your people's hearts.'
' You are breaking your own people's hearts, Nikolai
Vasilievich,' I ventured.
' Exactly,' rejoined Nick. (He hardly looked old enough
to warrant the dignity of ' Nikolai Vasilievich.') ' I have
broken enough hearts. I don't want to break any more.
I've had enough of this heart-breaking business, I can tell
you. It is enough to break your own.'

' Your Oscar Wilde,' Zina turned to me, ' said that hearts were made to be broken.'

' He also said,' I retorted, ' that " We all kill the thing we love," and, in fact, a few other expensive things of that sort. But it is no reason, I assure you, why you should break anybody's heart.'

' Exactly,' said Nicholas. ' You think it very jolly to live together without being married, don't you ? But you just ask Fanny Ivanovna how she feels about it. No, my child, your Oscar Wilde is a fool.'

Quite automatically we turned into a cinema, the Parisiana in the Nevski, and witnessed the sort of stuff to which an uncomplaining public is still being treated every day and night all over the globe. When Nicholas left the box to get some chocolates Zina put her white-gloved hand on my arm. ' I know,' she said, ' Nikolai is being made to appear a blackguard by people who misunderstand his complex personality, but I am ready to give my life for him, Andrei Andreiech. Oh, you have no idea what a thoroughly good man he is when he is away from all those petty worries, those mean jealousies, those paltry domestic squabbles, those innumerable families all hanging round his neck, and he, alone, standing up against those legions, yes, *legions* of relatives and dependants and hangers-on. Oh, don't laugh. I'm not excepting my own people. Oh, no ! I am indeed ashamed, Andrei Andreiech, that it should be so. I had a dream last night. Shall I tell you what it was ? It was Nikolai standing high upon a mountain peak, seeking to escape towards light and freedom and finding that he could not, because he was linked to the past. He tried to break the chains, but the past held him, clung to him, a monster with a thousand arms, like that picture in Gogol's *Terrible Vengeance*. He found the past too strong for him.

' Why can't he break with the past ? Why should the past always hold him ? Why should he always bear the burden of these families ? Andrei Andreiech ! he hasn't *lived* yet. For was that life ? I want to help him, make him happy, rid

him of these petty worries, these mean intrigues. I want
to help, to help, to help. But how can I help ?... I thought,
all night I thought out solutions, and then I came to what
seemed to me the one reasonable, the only just solution. I
proposed that we should commit suicide together. But,
Andrei Andreiech, he doesn't seem to be very keen on it.
Poor boy, with all these ugly worries he is becoming horribly
materialistic.'

They took me that evening to see Zina's people. They
lived across the river, over on the Petersburg side, a very
large family in a small flat. There were innumerable aunts
and uncles, sisters-in-law, second cousins, and such-like
relatives, and of course a collection of giggling flappers
practising the piano ; two ancient grandfathers—the oldest
thing in veterans—who had outlived their welcome, whose
deaths, in fact, were looked forward to with undisguised
impatience and freely discussed at meals ; and a middle-aged
doctor, his own health no better for his profession, with only a
poor practice to support that swarm; and Nikolai Vasilievich,
the mine-owner, standing behind them all like a benediction.

In addition there was Uncle Kostia, who, from what I
could see, was living on the resources of his younger
brother, Zina's father. Uncle Kostia was a writer. Yet,
though he had attained middle age, Uncle Kostia had never
published a line. His two departments were history and
philosophy, and every one in the family had the greatest
respect for Uncle Kostia and thought him very clever. Later
I had occasion to observe Uncle Kostia at closer range. He
would wake up extremely late and would then sit for hours
on his bed, thinking. He did not communicate his thoughts
to anybody else ; but all the members of the family took
it for granted that Uncle Kostia was very clever. Uncle
Kostia rarely dressed and rarely washed. When at length
he parted with his bed he would stroll about through all the
rooms in his dressing-gown, and think. No one spoke to
him because, for one thing, all were frightened of displaying
their ignorance in conversation, for Uncle Kostia was very

clever, and also, I think, because they were loth to interrupt
the flow of Uncle Kostia's thoughts. At length he would
settle down at a writing-table near the window in his
brother's study, and then for a long time Uncle Kostia would
rub his eyes. In a languid manner he would dip his pen into
ink and his hand would proceed to sketch diagrams and
flowers on the margin of his foolscap, and Uncle Kostia
would stare long at the window. Perhaps a buzzing fly
endeavouring to find an exit would arrest his flow of
thoughts, or would promote them—who knows ?—but
Uncle Kostia would grow very still : and one by one the
members of the family would leave the room on tiptoe, and
the last one out would shut the door behind him noiselessly.
For Uncle Kostia was writing. What he wrote no one knew ;
he had never breathed a word about it to anyone. All we
knew was that Uncle Kostia was very clever. From what I
could make out no one had ever seen a line of his writing.
But that he thought a great deal there was no question. His
life was spent in contemplation. But what it was he
contemplated, equally no one knew.

Such was the family to which Nikolai Vasilievich extended
his protectorate.

' He is such a really good man,' confided Zina's mother,
a grey-haired, God-fearing old lady. 'And to be pursued by
those two wicked women both bent on making his life
miserable, those cold and heartless daughters who laugh at
him . . . their own father ! Andrei Andreiech, our lives are
muddled up enough, God forgive us, and none of us knows
where he is or how he stands or what he is about ; but
there are things that in our hearts we know we mustn't do.
And for his own daughters to go spying on their father,
God forgive me, is the very limit. Just think of it, Andrei
Andreiech, just think of it ! Last Sunday, Zina tells me, she
was about to meet Nikolai in the Summer Garden, and—can
you imagine it ?—his two daughters—I forget which two—
with that Baron of theirs, followed them, pursued them
wherever they went, giggling all the while as loud as they

could, giggling... Nikolai and Zina were finally compelled
to board a tram-car to escape their pursuit. He wept when
he came to me, Andrei Andreiech, and I have never seen
Nikolai weep before. He said he hadn't thought it possible
of his daughters, Andrei Andreiech.'

After a somewhat sketchy dinner we all decided to go to
the Saburov Theatre to see a new play. We proceeded
accordingly in four cabs and settled down in three boxes.

About half-way through the first act I perceived Nikolai
give a start and then grow pale. I followed his gaze and
then looked straight before me. In a box almost opposite
our own sat Fanny Ivanovna, Sonia, Nina, Vera, Kniaz, and
Baron Wunderhausen. For some absurd reason I, too, felt
guilty and uncomfortable to the last degree, almost as if I
had been caught red-handed in some disreputable act.
Whether the silly play bored them and they were, like us,
disgusted with the characteristic utterances of some well-
to-do ex-student in the play holding forth on the disillusionment of life, or whether the sight of the prodigal Nicholas
in his congenial surroundings was too much for Fanny
Ivanovna ; but they all left the theatre before the curtain
fell on the second act.

Nikolai Vasilievich seemed unusually morose as we drove
home that night through the deserted streets of Petersburg.
' The most perplexing thing about it all, Andrei Andreiech,'
said he, ' is . . . well, it's like that fable of Krilov.' And he
quoted the fable with that curious pride that Russians usually
take in Krilov's un-Russian (I think British) common sense,
as he instanced the case of the load pulled jointly by the
swan, the crab and the pike in their several characteristically
individual directions with the distressing result—the moral !
—that the load, the fabulist tells us, is to-day exactly where
it was before they had started on their expedition. The
paradox of Nikolai's position was that he had fled from his
many family responsibilities to this engaging flapper precisely because of the intolerable burden of so many responsibilities—and had incurred additional ones.

## X

Now when I ask myself how I could have so hopelessly misgauged the situation, I find it difficult to give a clear account of it. I had wanted to help, to be a friend to all those helpless, charming and kind-hearted people... Anyhow, it was my first experience of ' intervention.'

That night I lay awake in bed, planning how I could straighten out the tangle. Was it not, I pondered, up to me, their mutual confidant, to see that these childish, fascinating people did not destroy each other's lives in their muddle-headedness and inertia? The older people had all blundered. Nina had been on a mission to Moscow, and Nina had failed. They would trust me, I said, to act for the best. And was it not a worthy task to save these helpless creatures from so much misery and anguish? Well, of course it was. Suddenly I felt violently enthusiastic. I felt so violently enthusiastic that I jumped out of bed. I paced the floor that midnight hour, thinking with a Napoleonic concentration.

I felt, as my thoughts ran ahead of me, that the *dramatis personæ* of this human drama was much too long to enable me to assign successfully to each character the part he was to play in his colleagues' lives. I switched on the light over my writing-table and began to write. I wrote down their names in two columns. Then I perceived that the two columns did not serve my purpose ; so I drew arrows and circles round the names and endeavoured to arrange them in sets and groups according to my own ideas as to how they should be mated. I began by mating Nina with myself. This was easy enough : it was obvious. I consented to make Baron Wunderhausen a present of Sonia. That was done. Obviously Kniaz would have to go on living on Nikolai Vasilievich till some employment could be found for him. I should have to go into this question later ; examine the shares, see what possibilities they had of ever going up, and

so on. Now so much was settled. Of course, Magda
Nikolaevna must have her divorce. No useful purpose
would be served by putting spokes in her wheel, by hinder-
ing her in her praiseworthy intention to marry Cecedek,
that Austrian fellow, who was extraordinarily wealthy. They
wanted all the money they could get. But the condition of
this concession should be that Cecedek must agree to share
the brunt of supporting the multitudinous families, dependants and hangers-on with Nikolai Vasilievich until such
time at least as something more definite could be known
about the mines. It might be advisable to sell the mines and
re-purchase the mortgaged house in the Mohovaya. But
that was a detail that could be settled later. I felt that I was
getting on marvellously.

Now that Nicholas and Magda were divorced (I could
not help calling them by their Christian names, for I felt so
much older and wiser than they, having taken them in hand),
Nicholas must be prevailed upon to marry Fanny. This step
would do much to relieve the tension and prevent bad blood
between the two. It would secure Fanny's prestige in her
own eyes and would consolidate her position in regard to
her people in Germany. Now, Fanny having been granted
this very liberal concession, which after all was nothing short
of her one real great ambition in life, she on her part should
not be allowed to impede Zina's passionate desire to live
with Nicholas : a gratification, as a matter of fact, demanded by the overpowering love of two human beings ;
and Zina, who had always been prepared for anything from
suicide upwards, would not begrudge Fanny the formal and
somewhat hollow superiority of wedlock ; while Zina's
people, in the face of the considerable financial assistance
that they would continue to receive at the hands of Nikolai
and Magda's future husband, would find that their objection
carried little moral weight. There remained Vera. She
should stay, provisionally, with Fanny Ivanovna and
Nicholas, the latter spending as much time in Fanny's household as might be deemed fit or practicable. Vera hated her

father, and Eisenstein, poor as he was, would not be likely to demand his daughter. Now Eisenstein should not be left without a job. He must leave the Stock Exchange. That was absolutely necessary. His dental qualifications should be looked into ; and he might—but that at any rate was not of the first importance—be made assistant to Zina's father (though unfortunately the latter's practice was all too small already). How to enlarge the practice could be settled afterwards. Uncle Kostia's manuscripts would have to be examined, and possibly some of his deeper thoughts might be published with advantage.

Now, having made these few preliminary arrangements, it was imperative to ensure the financial working of this new combine. Well, expenses must be cut down all round. Nicholas and Cecedek should not be taxed too heavily, for if they went bankrupt then the whole new structure would collapse like a pack of cards. I would set myself, at an early date, to examine very carefully the requirements of the various families and hangers-on.

First, there was Fanny's family in Germany. Now Fanny, once definitely married to Nicholas, should have more moral courage to face the situation. Those spendthrift brothers in the Guards must be told to chuck the army and enter a commercial life. Militarism was no honourable profession. The sisters should marry. For all I knew they might long ago have married men with considerable means, but have kept it quiet from their sister, so as to continue to draw allowances from Nicky.

Now Zina's family came next. The number of its mere hangers-on was preposterous. Of course, those two ancient grandfathers were already tottering and their end was nigh. The flappers who strummed on the piano were growing up. A few of them might be conveniently married off to suitable and financially independent young men. Zina's father, assisted by Eisenstein, might make a better job of his doctoring ; though to begin with, he should receive medical treatment himself.

Then...

I thought. There was no 'then.' I had disposed of them all. There were indeed fewer cases than I had expected. I had disposed of them as I had gone along. Of course, Baron Wunderhausen, after he had married Sonia, was not really disposed of, perhaps on the contrary. But this was an isolated case into which I need not enter, at any rate just yet.

Perhaps I was young and absurd. But *was* I absurd? What was wrong with my proposition? What thoughtful mind would accuse me of absurdity if it only cared to look at the thing squarely? The people were helpless—children.

Of course, I would have to do it all tactfully, slowly, discreetly. But really, was it not a worthy mission? To arbitrate; to *settle* things. I felt as President Wilson must have felt years later when he was laying down the principles of a future League of Nations.

I stood before Nina the following day, bursting with the desire to lay it all down before her, all in a heap, as it were, but holding myself back with an effort, conscious of the danger of precipitate action. 'Let us sit down, Nina,' I said, fingering a large folded sheet of paper. I held another even larger sheet, rolled up under my arm. 'You see, Nina, we young people must help the old people out of their muddles. They are obviously unfit to help themselves.'

'I have done what I could,' she answered. 'I have been down to Moscow, but of course I admit I only acted as Fanny Ivanovna's envoy.'

'Exactly. You have failed?'

'I didn't enjoy plenipotentiary powers, as they call it.'

'Quite so. Now listen to me, Nina.' And I proceeded to lay before her the principles on which I said I was going to re-shape their lives : each one would have to give up something for the benefit of the whole, and each one would similarly receive a compensation of some kind in that future life of theirs : in short, as I had mapped it out the night before. I now unfolded my chart and diagram, and she bent over them and our heads nearly touched as we went into

this complicated question very thoroughly and seriously
indeed. I could barely suppress the look of pride that every
now and then would steal over my face. I explained and
propounded with something of the insolence of a creator,
an artist and a prophet, and she listened to me, all absorbed
in my scheme, following the diagram, I thought, with
marvellous intuition.

'Ah, yes. I understand,' she murmured. 'That's good.
This couldn't be better. Ah, there you kill two birds with
one stone . . . oh, three birds ! '

Then Nina rose.

'Well, what d'you think of it ? ' I said with undisguised
triumph in my look. And looking at me with a quaint and
sudden seriousness that astonished me immensely (to the
detriment of my triumphant look), she answered :

'All this is very well, but . . . pray what *business is it all
of yours ?* '

I expostulated. I told her how eager I had been to help.
But she laughed. She made fun of me. She had been making
fun of me all the time, even while we were bending with
such a serious mien over the chart and diagram. And I
perceived that her serious look, her interest in the scheme
a while ago, was all deliberately put on to commit me more
deeply to the exposition of my scheme in order to make
more fun of me afterwards.

She laughed. She burst with merriment.

'Nina ! '

She laughed still more. She was convulsed ; she could
barely speak, and the tears came into her eyes.

Then she opened the door into the corridor and called out.

'Sonia ! Sonia ! '

'Nina ! ' I cried in remonstrance.

'Vera ! ' she called. 'Papa ! Fanny Ivanovna ! Kniaz !
Pàvl Pàvlch ! '

I had to realize, to my deep shame and anguish, that they
were all at home, as they entered the room one by one. My
face grew crimson.

Nina held out the chart and the diagram at arm's length and explained, it seemed to me wilfully misrepresenting the whole thing, mating individuals in a preposterous fashion, so that Sonia would cry out :

' But Cecedek does not *want* to marry Fanny Ivanovna ! '

And Fanny Ivanovna, colouring highly, would exclaim : ' What—what's that ? '

' They more or less belong to the same race,' said Nina. ' Is that the idea ? ' She turned to me with assumed innocence.

And Sonia cried again, ' But Zina doesn't *want* to live with the dentist-Jew ! '

' I take it that she'll have to. You can't have it all ways, you know, in such a complicated scheme.' And then with a side look at me, ' Am I right ? '

' And why should Cecedek subsidize anybody ? '

' Why ? ' said Nina, with a look at me.

' You're making a farce of it ! ' I cried in utter desperation.

' It's you who are making a farce of it,' Nina cried. ' Papa, he is laughing at us ! '

Fanny Ivanovna walked out of the room in what seemed to me a defiant manner. I seemed to hear a solitary ' Hm ! '

Nikolai Vasilievich, with the diagram in his hand and trailing the chart in a degrading manner along the floor, so that I burnt with shame for my neat and able work of the night before, led me aside and said in a very earnest tone of voice, addressing me as ' Young man ? ' :

' You know we are always glad to have you here, but to make fun of our family difficulties . . . to make fun . . . to make fun . . . ' (he was getting a little heated) ' of our family difficulties into which you, as our guest, were unavoidably initiated . . . is, I consider, tactless and indelicate.' And he tore up first the chart and then the diagram into a thousand fragments and flung them into the great big stove in the corner of the room.

' Nikolai Vasilievich ! ' I cried. ' I assure you I only wanted to help.'

'Oh, look here,' said Nikolai Vasilievich impatiently, turning on his heels, 'please stop these unbecoming jokes. They're not even funny.' And they all left me.

But I went into the corridor and caught Nina by the hand and dragged her back into the room and did what is known as 'giving her a bit of my mind.' I was so wild that I did not know how to begin. 'Very well,' I cried at last, 'I shall leave you all to stew in your own juice!'

'Very well,' she said.

'And I shall never come again.'

'Very well,' she said.

And it seemed that to whatever I said in my excitement, she answered coldly and indifferently as she sat there, looking at me coldly and indifferently, 'Very well,' until it irritated me beyond endurance, and I cried:

'*Very well!* But do you silly people realize how utterly laughable you all are? Oh, my God! Can't you see yourselves?' (I could not see myself.) 'But can't you see that you have been lifted out of Chehov?... Oh, what would he not have given to see you and use you!'

'He's dead,' she said.

'But there are others. Oh, no, my dear, you are not safe. What's there to prevent some mean, unscrupulous scribbler, who cares less for people than for his art, from writing you up? One doesn't often come across such incomparable material. I feel I am almost capable of doing it myself. I'll write up such a Three Sisters as will knock old Chehov into a cocked hat. It's so easy. You just set down the facts. The only handicap that I'm aware of is that you are all of you so preposterously improbable that no one would believe that you were real. This is, in fact, the trouble with most modern literature. No fiction is good fiction unless it is true to life, and yet no life is worth relating unless it be a life out of the ordinary; and then it seems improbable like fiction.'

She did not answer, but by her face I could see that now she was angry.

'I wanted to help you, and this is the thanks I get.'

And feeling that I must make my exit dramatically con-
clusive, I said, 'And now I'm going'; and then on
reflection added, 'and I shall never come again.'

I lingered for a moment, to give her an opportunity of
stopping me. But she did not avail herself of it; and so I
left the room. Once or twice I stopped in the corridor to
listen if she was coming, when I intended to continue my
dramatic exit. But she did not come.

It did not matter, anyhow, I thought, as I was putting on
my coat (slowly while no one watched me, but if she had
appeared I would have hastened my withdrawal). I knew
that she would watch me from the window, and at the door
there stood that beautifully proportioned nag 'Professor
Metchnikoff,' waiting for me. My heart leapt within my
breast at the agreeable thought of how I would step into the
victoria and drive off swiftly with a dramatic conclusiveness.

I dashed down the staircase. I stood beneath the porch.
But where in heaven was Professor Metchnikoff?

And I beheld where he was.

I had often seen our wily Tartar coachman Alexei shake
his little head, as I lavished praise on the shape of Professor
Metchnikoff, and heard him say that the animal was 'un-
reliable.' I had never believed him. Well, did I now?

I beheld a curious spectacle. The little wily Alexei, big-
bottomed in accordance with the best traditions, sat helpless
on his soft broad box-seat and flapped his reins in a hopeless
fashion, producing with his lips an entreating but ineffectual
sound, as Professor Metchnikoff, composed and dignified,
retreated backwards toward the tramlines at the cross-roads.

I ran to his rescue, and taking Professor Metchnikoff by
the bridle I led him forward. I looked up as I did so. Thank
God, Nina was not at the window. I then left Professor
Metchnikoff, who stood quite quiet, and stepped into the
carriage. No sooner had I done so than Professor Metchnikoff resumed his steady and dignified retreat. The coachman,
strapped tightly in his cushioned clothes, was helpless as

a doll. I glanced at the house, and lo ! on the balcony above
Nina's window there stood Sonia, Nina, Vera, Kniaz,
Fanny Ivanovna, Nikolai Vasilievich, and Baron Wunder-
hausen, looking down at me and laughing.

I glanced up at them and crimsoned, and then in a fury
I leant forward and hit Professor Metchnikoff across the
back with my walking-stick. Professor Metchnikoff halted
for a moment, as if considering what to do, and then
decided in favour of a retirement. And, seated in the open
carriage, I retreated steadily to the accompaniment of
laughter from the balcony. Despite the coachman's frantic
efforts to the contrary, I vanished backwards very slowly
out of sight—when suddenly the fiendish nag jerked forward
and trotted home as though nothing had ever been the
matter.

## XI

How often then I dreamed of those white nights of
Petersburg, those white mysterious sleepless nights...

Fanny Ivanovna was alone, and we sat together on the
open balcony and talked about her troubles in the white
night. We sat listless. We felt a strange tremor. We waited
for the night, for twilight ; but they were not. Heaven had
come down over earth. It was one splash of humid, milk-
white, pellucid mist. We could see everything before us
clearly to the minutest detail. The street with its tall buildings tried hard to fall asleep, but could not : it, too, suffered
from insomnia ; and the black window-panes of the sleepless houses were like tired eyes of great monsters. Now and
then a man would pass beneath us, his steps resounding
sharp and loud upon the pavement. Curiously, he had no
shadow. Then he was gone, and there was not a soul in the
street.

A horrible dream crept over us... And to rouse ourselves
from its increasing domination, we talked. Talking with
her, as ever, meant listening. ' I have passed the tragic stage,

Andrei Andreiech,' she said. 'Now I don't care. I am almost accustomed to my position.'

I tried to put a word in. 'I suggest, Fanny Ivanovna, that you all break loose, disentangle yourselves from one another, and then begin at the beginning.'

But she talked on into the night, heedless of my remarks.

'I am only waiting till Nikolai Vasilievich can pay me off; then I shall return to Germany. I am indeed quite optimistic. I am now at the laughing stage. You see, our life can hardly be called a comedy, for if it were produced on the stage no one would believe it was real. No real people could be so silly. It is a farce, Andrei Andreiech. You were right when you made a farce of it then with your chart and diagram and things, do you remember?'

'I honestly wished to help,' I remonstrated.

But she laughed appreciatively, as if to say that she had noted with approval my attempt to pull her leg.

She talked in fragments. 'Yes, Andrei Andreiech, you will find—it is indeed a curious thing—that girls who are brought up in such unnatural surroundings as you would think scarcely contributive to the development of the moral virtues, are often the very girls who have the strictest possible conception of morality. What they have seen around them has only had the effect of putting them upon their guard. They are morally inoculated. I haven't the slightest hesitation in allowing them to read any books they like. They can read Verbitskaya and Artsibashev and Lappo-Danilevskaya and the rest of them if they please. You in England are fortunate indeed. You have serious, moral writers who think of the good of the race and really teach you something positive, constructive and worth while. You have Byron and Oscar Wilde.'

Like so many other people in Russia, Fanny Ivanovna believed that England has three great outstanding writers: Byron, Shakespeare, and Oscar Wilde.

'*Ach!* Andrei Andreiech! I have had a terrible row

with Cecedek. It's all that Baron Wunderhausen. He made
love to Nina...'

I remember that at these words I sat up in my chair.

'. . . in French, Andrei Andreiech!

'"I hate talking of *such* things in Russian," he said,
thinking he would impress her. But she wouldn't listen.'

My body relaxed in the chair.

'If there's one thing that Nina simply cannot stand, it
is being made love to . . . above all in French! He came
to me after that and said:

'"Fanny Ivanovna, it came over me like that . . . overnight!..."

'"Oh, then it will go out overnight," I said. "Pàvel
Pàvlovich, please don't talk of it to me." But he turned to
me and said in a secretive whisper:

'"Fanny Ivanovna, if you will help me to win her heart
I will be your greatest friend on earth." And then, after
the manner of a doctor, "And now tell me all your troubles.
We'll see what we can do."

'"Pàvel Pàvlovich," I cried, "*Sie sind verrückt*. My
troubles are my private affairs and concern no one but
myself. Good night."

'So he complained of me to Magda Nikolaevna; and,
would you believe it! she sent Cecedek to tell me that she
will not allow me to hamper her daughters' happiness, that
she doesn't want them to die old maids, like me—*me*! if
you please—that I am unfit to look after them, and so on,
and so on. Andrei Andreiech, they are sixteen, fifteen and
fourteen! But I can guess the true cause. She wants to
marry Cecedek and she naturally doesn't want her daughters
to live with her as this would make her appear her own age,
to say nothing of the danger of his falling in love with one
of them. They are so pretty.'

'But why need they live with her at all?'

'Ah,' said Fanny Ivanovna. 'She said emphatically that
she will not have them live with their father if that's the
way he carries on. She is afraid it will corrupt their morals.'

'But doesn't she continue to draw an allowance from Nikolai Vasilievich?'

'She does. But ever since she met Cecedek, who is preposterously rich, she has lost her faith in Nikolai Vasilievich's mines—indeed says so openly. This distresses Nikolai very much indeed. I don't know why it is that he attaches such importance to her faith in the mines, unless it is because he acquired those gold-mines in her time. Of course, she is anxious for her daughters' future. She feels that their chances are getting spoiled with her own life and that of Nikolai Vasilievich becoming muddled up. I don't doubt that she loves her daughters and means well.

'So now our Baron is again after Sonia, but really after the mines, if you ask me.' She laughed a little, privately, to herself, and then said, 'I wish he'd wash his neck...

'Soon, very soon, Andrei Andreiech, I shall leave them. It will be hard . . . intolerably hard. But my mind is made up. I am not such a fool, Andrei Andreiech, as not to know when my time is up. And then I have a little pride still left in me. It is now merely a matter of the mines. I am ready. I have begun to pack. I have written home to Germany. But I couldn't post the letter. Not yet... Andrei Andreiech: what have I to live for? Will you tell me: *what?*... Only when I am gone from them perhaps the children will say: " She has been good to us. She has loved us like a mother " —and then, perhaps, I shall not have lived in vain.'

I went home by the silent river. The Fortress of St. Peter and St. Paul was like a weary watchman. The Admiralty Needle seemed lost in the white mist. I sat down on a stone seat of the embankment and rested. The broad milky river was so mysteriously calm in the granite frame of the quays. I sat and wondered; then my thoughts began to drift; and I was lost in this half light, this half dream, this unreal half existence.

# PART II

THE REVOLUTION

# I

THEN I went to Oxford, and when the war broke out I joined the Navy. But just before the revolution, Admiral Butt, who had gone on a special mission to Russia, applied for my 'Anglo-Russian' services.

I still remember very vividly the morning following on my arrival in Petrograd, when I had to meet the Admiral for the first time at the British Embassy. I ascended the broad staircase with its worn red carpet to the Chancery. Very perfect young men, very perfectly dressed, were conversing in very perfect intonations about love among monkeys. It struck me as delightfully human for diplomatists. When I descended, the Admiral had not yet arrived. I talked to Yuri, the hall-porter, a clean-shaven individual of uncertain nationality, violently pro-British, and speaking several languages all very badly. Every now and then the great heavy door would open—it was snowing heavily outside—and some man or woman would come in and inquire if this was the Military District Staff. 'It is the British Embassy,' replied Yuri proudly. And he explained the error. The Military District Staff was 4 Palace Square; the Embassy 4 Palace Quay. In peace-time people did come in occasionally and inquire if this was the Military District Staff; but since war had been declared they seemed to be doing little else. I pondered over the possibility of Yuri, unable one day to withstand the increasing pressure of inquiries, going mad and holding forth on this subject to his brother inmates henceforth indefinitely in a lunatic asylum.

Helping me on with my coat, Yuri was suddenly seized by a strange panic. He dropped the coat on the floor and dashed to the door. I followed him, thinking it was the revolution. I was rewarded for my exertion. The Ambassador's car drove up, and sitting in it were Sir George

Buchanan and the French Ambassador. Yuri sprang up and pulling off his cap opened the door of the vehicle and stood still in a paroxysm of reverence and awe. But the two great men within continued talking, the Frenchman in that agitated, agile manner that Frenchmen have, the Englishman with a fine superiority of distinction. The Ambassadors of the two friendly powers sat talking, evidently unaware that they had arrived. Yuri held the door open, still bareheaded, the incarnation of servility and devotion. Then they entered. Yuri made a dash for Sir George's feet, and began hastily to unbuckle his felt goloshes, while the great diplomatist with his fur collar still up to his temples and his round fur cap cocked over one ear stood panting in his great fur coat. I had an absurd idea that something great must be happening on the political horizon.

Finally the Admiral arrived. He was a tall, imperious figure. His movements were powerful and sweeping. He had the air of a man engaged in winning the war while everybody else about him was obstructing him in his patriotic task. His voice was the voice of such a man. His look seemed specially selected to match his voice. That war-winning quality was clearly manifest in his personality, but his actual work towards that end was all very obscure.

Then one morning, as I was about to cross the Troitski Bridge to meet the Admiral, I was stopped by the police and was compelled to go home and change into uniform. When I returned the revolution had already broken out. The Admiral had just witnessed the sacking of the Arsenal by a disorderly crowd. Regiment after regiment was going over to the revolution. Solitary shots, and now and then machine-gun fire, were heard from various quarters of the city. The Admiral and I stood at the window and watched. Lorry after lorry packed with armed soldiery and workmen, some lying in a ' ready ' attitude along the mudguards, went past us in a kind of wild and dazzling joy ride, waving red flags and revolutionary banners to shouts of ' Hurrah ! ' from the crowds in the street. The Admiral stood with his hands folded on the window-sill, unable to withhold his enthusiasm. It was a clear, bright day, I think, and very cold.

That evening following the outbreak of the revolution was vividly impressed upon my memory. During the day I had listened to innumerable speeches, some of a Liberal loftiness; others of a menacingly proletarian character, threatening death to capital and revolution to the world at large. There was a tendency to flamboyant extravagance and exaggeration. ' Down with Armies and Navies ! ' shouted one speaker hysterically. ' Down with militarism ! Through red terror to peace, freedom and brotherhood ! ' There were placards and banners and processions. ' Land and Liberty ! ' was a popular watchword. Red was the dominant colour, and the opening bars of the Marseillaise were a kind of recurring *Leitmotiv* in the tumult. Crossing a bridge I passed a company of soldiers newly revolted. They marched alert and joyous to the sound of some old familiar marching songs till they came to the words ' for the Czar.' Having sung these words they stopped somewhat abruptly and perplexed. ' *How* for the Czar ? ' one of them asked. ' *How* for the Czar ? ' they repeated, looking at each other sheepishly. Then they marched on without singing. There were peasants who did not know the word ' revolution ' and thought it was a woman who would supersede the Czar. Others wanted a republic with a czar. And there were others still who interpreted the word republic as ' rezshpublicoo,' thinking that it meant ' cut up the public.' In the Troitski Square I was stopped by a young enthusiastic Russian officer who, attracted by my British uniform, spoke to me in English, his eyes glittering with excitement. ' Sir,' he said, ' you now will have more vigorous Allies.' And then in the Nevski I passed a procession of Anarchists who are regarded by the Bolsheviks with about the same degree of unmitigated horror as the Bolsheviks are regarded by the *Morning Post*. They marched with a gruesome look about their faces, bearing their horrible colours of black, crested with a human skull and cross-bones.

And somewhat later in the day I sat at dinner with Zina's people on the Petrograd side, and the presence of a score of students, male and female, an engineer, a lawyer, and a journalist or two, all of that revolutionary intelligentsia, probably accounted for the Liberal atmosphere that prevailed. Yesterday they had been revolutionaries; to-day they were contented Liberals, hailing Lvov and Miliukov as the heroes of the day. The engineer drank to the future : ' The old world is dead : long live the new world ! '

The two ancient grandfathers were much too old and feeble to intervene on behalf of the old order of things ; they had exhausted their Liberal aspirations with the liberation of the serfs in 1861 and could not see what in the world more anybody wanted. Zina's father, underpaid and ill as he was, had lost for ever the hope of seeing better days, and failed to see how the revolution could affect his own position, Nikolai Vasilievich was still keeping him so far. These Liberals interpreted the revolution as a protest against the pro-German tendency at court, and as an attempt to get into line with the Western Democracies in this hitherto unconvincing struggle against militarism and autocracy. The news was rumoured that the Czar had abdicated. Again, it was said that a section of the court had been planning a revolution to depose the Emperor and substitute his brother Michael in order to carry on the war more vigorously ; and that the people's revolution had preceded it by two days. Some monarchists now wanted to put down the revolution in order to carry on the war ; other monarchists wanted to put down the war in order to put down the revolution ; and still other monarchists wanted to put down the revolution and did not care a hang about the war. The Liberals wanted the revolution to carry on the war ; the Czar wanted to put down the revolution ; the Socialists and workmen wanted to put down the war and to put down the Czar ; and the soldiers and sailors wanted to put down their officers. The Liberal gathering drank to Russia's Allies ;

and then Uncle Kostia, obviously moved by the great event, rose and said in a slow, melodious voice :

' We shall not talk about or criticize the past. We shall carry it gently into the depths of the garden and bury it there among the flowers. And then, carefully, we shall look into the cradle and nurse very tenderly the slumbering future.'

This attitude, we all felt, was befitting to the great bloodless revolution.

## II

I remember the excitement of it all. Uncle Kostia, it appeared, had risen earlier that day on account of the revolution ; and after dinner, still in his dressing-gown and slippers, he paced the floor quicker than was his custom, and, contrary to his practice, discoursed at great length. He held that history was moving at an unheard-of pace, and he complained that it was indeed difficult for him, an historian, to keep pace with it. The revolution had overtaken Uncle Kostia as he was still tackling the age of Anne.

From Zina's house I remember walking to the Bursanovs' in the Mohovaya. I passed the sombre silhouettes of the snow-covered barges frozen on the Neva. It was dark now and the crowds in the streets were more tumultuous. Soldiers and civilians alike walked aimlessly, rifle slung over the shoulder. Several wine-cellars had been broken into ; there were drunkards in the streets ; but anyhow, all seemed drunk with the revolution. Shots were heard every now and then, mostly fired in the air, while the law courts had gone up in flames. The revolution, it was felt, had been established.

Curiously enough I had not seen the Bursanovs on my return to Petrograd until that night. They were just the same. Kniaz sat in the corner of the little drawing-room in his usual chair, and it seemed that the revolution had impressed him. But how it had impressed him no one could have divined. Need I say that the three sisters sat in much the same positions, waiting—waiting for developments? Nikolai Vasilievich was very bitter. He had regarded the war almost as a deliberate attempt of providence to complicate his already very complicated domestic situation, and considering that providence had had the satisfaction of achieving its pernicious end, it seemed he could not understand the necessity of a revolution. ' Malignity ! Malignity ! ' he muttered, lowering the blinds, as if to show that he, at any rate, would have nothing to do with it.

' Nothing noble about it at all ! ' he answered me.

And Fanny Ivanovna, who had been sitting silently for some time, looked as if she were entirely of his opinion on that point.

And then a horrible groan was heard from the adjoining room. I cast a swift interrogative glance at Nikolai Vasilievich. I had an idea that they had hidden some wretched half-mutilated policeman, the victim of a revolutionary mob. But Nikolai Vasilievich and Fanny Ivanovna looked awkward and ashamed. There was, I noticed, a kind of appeal for sympathy in their eyes.

' That is Fanny Ivanovna's husband,' said Nikolai Vasilievich apologetically.

I looked incredulous, and he explained. As Fanny Ivanovna was not married to him, she was a German subject, and when war broke out she was to go back to Germany or be interned in Vologda. She refused to go to Germany till Nikolai Vasilievich had provided for her for life, but as the war had further crippled his finances he was not in a position to give her the money ; so they married her to Eberheim, an elderly gentleman of German extraction but a Russian subject. As his nominal wife Fanny Ivanovna was a Russian subject and could live in Russia until such time as the improvement in the working of the gold-mines made it possible for Nikolai Vasilievich to provide for her for life. Then if he could get a divorce from his wife he would marry Zina.

' Is he wounded ? ' I asked, scenting revolutionary blood in the air.

' No—cancer,' said Nikolai Vasilievich. And contrasted with this word painted red, the revolution out of doors seemed pale and trifling.

' He is going to have an operation in a day or so.'

' Has he suffered long ? ' I inquired.

' Oh, we took him out of hospital,' explained Fanny Ivanovna. ' You may think it odd, but he consented to the marriage on condition that we took him home and looked after him. He said that he would not live long in any case and that money was no earthly use to him in his condition : what he wanted was care and comfort. And now the doctors and operations are costing Nikolai Vasilievich a good bit of money, I can tell you. Really, we are most unfortunate people... And Sonia, too, marrying Baron Wunderhausen, who, as I suspected, is a drag on Nikolai Vasilievich's resources. Really, he cannot afford it, Andrei Andreiech. The mines——' She waved her hand. Nikolai Vasilievich, with his hands deep in his trouser pockets, stood looking at the window, though the blinds were lowered and there was nothing he could see.

' The wedding ceremony,' she went on, ' was painful. I barely stood it myself. The priest at first refused to marry us. Nikolai Vasilievich had to lead him aside and bribe him. Eberheim's condition was so bad—critical. It was wicked.— Yet he has a way of lasting. He has lasted now for over two years. One wants to be human to him, but really, Andrei Andreiech, look at us, look at us—us. And now the revolution. Who *wants* the revolution ? ' She put her chin on her hand and turned her face away. There was silence.

Then, suddenly, without reason or provocation, she turned on the old Kniaz, sitting neatly in his usual armchair, imperturbable like a butler :

' Kniaz ! Don't sit there like that, like... Oh, God, you've

been sitting like that in that chair for thirteen years——
Say something ! Say something ! '

' What can I say ? ' he smiled faintly.

' What can you say ! ' she echoed ; and again there was
silence.

' Hasn't he got any relations ? ' I asked.

She shook her head.

' No money ? '

' Penniless.'

' Is he...good ? '

' Yes, but...exacting.'

' Oh, poor fellow, he can't help it,' said Nikolai Vasilievich.

' Poor fellow,' said Fanny Ivanovna.

' Poor fellow,' I echoed.

For a moment we sat in silence. We waited for Eberheim
to groan again ; but he too was silent ; and we could just
hear the measured ticking of the great oak-panelled clock
in the corner and the subdued tumult of the streets below.

' And where is Magda Nikolaevna ? ' I asked.

' She is with Cecedek.'

' One burden less, what, Nikolai Vasilievich ? '

Nikolai Vasilievich sighed.

' You would hardly say so,' said Fanny Ivanovna, ' for
Nikolai Vasilievich still has to keep his wife.'

' But what of Cecedek ? '

' I am very sorry for him,' said Fanny Ivanovna.

And I learnt that at the outbreak of hostilities the Russian
authorities had found it necessary to confiscate the whole
of Cecedek's property. They were then going to intern him,
but he succeeded in proving to them that he was now a
Czech ; and so they set him free. But the property which
they had taken from him as an Austrian they did not return
to him as a Czech. He had been in correspondence with
the authorities on this subject ever since July, 1914, and on
his ultimate success in getting some of it refunded his
marriage with Magda Nikolaevna must henceforth depend.
Whether the revolution would assist him in his ambitious

expectations, or would delay them further, it was hard to prophesy. Nikolai Vasilievich helped him as much as he was able in his present circumstances. In the meantime Magda Nikolaevna had suspended her application for a divorce and was still on Nikolai Vasilievich's books for payment. But Cecedek's attitude had not changed. He now rather liked to emphasize the Slavic side to their union, had in the last three years developed a Czech intonation in his Russian speech, professed an undue regard for his ' Brother-Slavs,' pronounced his own name ' Chechedek,' and in signing put those funny little accents on the C's.

I left them very early next morning ; in the excitement of the day there had been much work left overnight un-accomplished. It was about six o'clock when I crossed the Field of Mars. Soldiers in odd groups strolled along in the snow, now and then firing off a rifle in the air, just for the fun of the thing ; and the capital wore that appearance of a banqueting-hall in the shrewd light of the morning after a particularly heavy feast. Fretful clouds moved swiftly across the winter sky. The morning promised a fine day.

### III

The revolution dragged on through the winter and ' deepened ' as the months advanced. The forerunners of confusion became visible : food and commodities were being procured in an irregular manner. All were waiting.

Pictures of them recur continually to my mind, as I write. I can see Fanny Ivanovna, and particularly I can see the three sisters, always sitting in the same positions, perched on sundry chairs and sofas, Fanny Ivanovna engaged in silent contemplation over needlework, and Kniaz sitting in his usual chair, reading, or more often sitting idly, thinking into space. The seasons would be changing rapidly from one to the other—but their position never ! Rain would drum against the window-pane, snow would be falling on the street below ; then the ice on the Neva would begin to break and slowly move toward the Bay ; and again one would feel the onset of spring, the unfolding of white nights.

' How tiring this is, Andrei Andreiech,' Fanny Ivanovna complained. ' To be always waiting to begin to *live*. When is that upward movement in happiness, that splendid life that we are always waiting for, to begin at last ? Somehow you wait for the spring. But spring has come . . . *alone*, and only emphasizes our misery, by the contrast.—Spring makes me mad. I begin to want impossible things...'

' You are an active woman, Fanny Ivanovna. You ought not to sit still. It's bad for you. You ought to run about.'

' But—I've got to wait.'

' I suppose waiting is sitting still. It *is*, in a sense.'

' It isn't that. But what am I going to run about for ? I go out shopping. But that doesn't *advance* things, you understand. Besides, I simply dread asking Nikolai Vasilievich for money.'

' He hasn't got any ? '

' He has. He's always borrowing—*crescendo, forte, fortissimo* ! But where will it end ? When ? Borrowing money is all right if you can do it. But it's not, as it were, an income ; it's not—how shall I put it ?—an end in itself, is it ? There's got to be something, somewhere, sometime. Those gold-mines have got to justify themselves. Our plans, our movements, everything depends on them. That's why it's so annoying. They've got to pay, and I am confident that they will pay. But *when* ? '

She rose abruptly, as was her wont, her black silk skirt rustling as she swept out.

It was ' Papa this ' and ' Mama that ' and ' Fanny Ivanovna the other thing.'

' Won't you stop sighing ? ' I suggested.

' It's all very well for you,' protested the three sisters simultaneously. ' But do you think it's very nice for us ? '

' What do you want, anyhow ? '

They did not answer; they looked at the window, brooding.

I said in a jovial tone of voice :

' Well, I tried to help you. But you won't be helped.'

' Helped us indeed ! ' they cried out simultaneously. The three sisters had a way of speaking simultaneously and almost word for word in matters of domestic politics. They were a party in themselves, stubbornly opposed to all the other camps of Nikolai Vasilievich's family.

The night before, I had taken them to Kusivitski's concert. People had been staring enviously at me, as if to ask : ' Who are those three pretty kittens ? ' I felt absurdly like a proud papa. The music was excruciating. During the piano solo I clung to my chair : I could scarcely sit still. ' Scriabin,' I burst out as the music stopped, ' is a persistent knocking at the door—but the door doesn't open. Still, as we might know in any case that there *is* nothing behind the door, that doesn't greatly matter, does it ? It's the knocking that is a human necessity. And what a desperate knocking it is ! '

Nina looked at me with that trick she had of assuming innocence and said : ' Which door ? '

And it flashed across my mind that, whereas Sonia played the piano with an agreeable touch of feeling, Nina's hammering was shrill and disagreeable, while, musically, Vera was still an unknown quantity.

But the pianist had resumed.

' What is this ? ' Nina asked.

' A fox-trot,' I replied, very superior.

I sat on the small seat facing the three sisters, as Professor Metchnikoff trotted homeward through the sombre streets. The night was warm and humid. By the street lamps I could see their faces. When she was silent Nina looked so wise. Perhaps she seemed wiser than she actually was. All this— the war, the revolution—she had overlooked : and it did not exist. Scriabin—she had overlooked him. And he did not exist. But she was there, watchful...

The day after was like the day before. They sat there listless—Fanny Ivanovna, Kniaz and the three sisters. The three sisters always sat in some extraordinary positions, on the backs of sofas and easy chairs, and Fanny Ivanovna and Kniaz sat in very ordinary positions. Nikolai Vasilievich alone was always absent ; and I think there was a sort of feeling running through us all that he at least was busy, *doing* something. But in more sceptical moods I know I was inclined to question dubiously whether he too was *getting* anywhere for all the semblance of activity that his mysterious absence involved. I remember the silhouette of Nina's profile at the window. I can feel the tension of the silence that hung over the room, the suspense of waiting—of indefinite waiting for indefinite things. In the hush that had crept upon us I could fancy I could sense acutely the disturbing presence of the things my eye could not behold : the gilded domes radiant in the fading sunlight, the many bridges thrown across the widespread stream ; and in the stillness I was made to feel as if by instinct the throbbing pulse of Petrograd. The leaden waves splashed gently against the granite banks ; and the air was full of that yearning melancholy call of life that yet reminds one—God knows why—of the imminence of death ; and in the sky there was the promise of a white night.

## IV

Petrograd looked thoroughly nasty on that cold November morning. There was the drizzling snow, and it was still dark as I walked home with Uncle Kostia. We had been at the Finland Station to see off two of Uncle Kostia's nieces who were going abroad. It was the morning of the Bolshevik Revolution, and Uncle Kostia looked pessimistic. ' Do you remember all those student-revolutionaries, the heroes of our young intelligentsia, who had been persecuted by the old régime ? Well,'—he pointed from the bridge that we were traversing to the Bolshevik craft that had arrived from Kronstadt overnight—' *this* is more than they bargained for. More than they bargained for.'

We walked on.

' They are malcontents again—but on the other side ! Truth is fond of playing practical jokes of this sort. My God ! how elusive it is. It is wonderful how beneath our hastily made-up truths, the truths of usage and convenience, there runs independently, often contrariwise, a wider, bigger truth. Can't you feel it ? The pseudo-reason of unreason. The lack of reasonable evidence in reason. Issues, motives being muddled up. This ethical confusion, and the blind habitual resort to bloodshed as a means of straightening it out. More confusion. Honour is involved. Bloodshed as a solution. More honour involved in the solution. More bloodshed. That idiotic plea that each generation should sacrifice itself for the so-called benefit of the next ! It never seems to end.—Oh, how the pendulum swings ! Wider and wider, and we are shedding blood generation after generation. For *what* ? For *whom* ?—For future generations ! My God, what fools we are ! Fools shedding blood for the sake of future fools, who will do as much ! '

' But what are you to do ? *What* ? ' I persisted.

Uncle Kostia was evasive. ' You see,' he said at last, ' subtleties of the mind, if pursued to their logical conclusions, become crudities. Let us cease our conversation at this point.'

Barricades appeared in the streets. Bridges were being suspended. Lorries of joy-riding proletarians became familiarly conspicuous, as I walked on towards the Bursanovs'.

I found the household in a state of wild excitement. However, the event had no connexion with the Revolution. In fact, with continual domestic revolutions in their own home, the much ado about the political revolution appeared, particularly to the three sisters, a foolish affectation.

I learnt that Nikolai Vasilievich had just discovered that his book-keeper Stanitski, at the instigation of his house-agent, had these last five years been falsifying the books and robbing him wholesale. When the discovery was made the house-agent had vanished into the darkness whence he had emerged. But as I entered I was very nearly knocked down by Nikolai Vasilievich dashing after Stanitski, the book-keeper, as he was flying down the stairs. He caught him by the tail of his overcoat and dragged him back into his study. He had him standing, stiff and awkward and ashamed, before his desk, while he himself reclined in his arm-chair.

Nikolai Vasilievich did not shout, as Stanitski, who knew his master intimately, had, no doubt, expected him to do. He spoke quietly and even sadly ; and it was the sadness of his speech that penetrated Stanitski's Slavic nature to the heart. ' How could you have cheated me like that, Ivan Sergeiech—me who have trusted you ? '

And Stanitski became emotional. ' Nikolai Vasilievich ! ' he exclaimed with his hands joined together and the whites of his eyes turned heavenwards. ' Nikolai Vasilievich ! God in Heaven knows I have not been helping myself to your money, as you seem to think, recklessly. But since I took a little—and I have a wife, children, dependants—I had to do what the house-agent told me. I was in his hands, at the mercy of a blackguard and a robber. Nikolai Vasilie-vich : I often felt I wanted to warn you of this rascal. But I was in his hands . . . since I took myself. But I took in measure, Nikolai Vasilievich, conscientiously, with my eyes on God.'

The old man sobbed bitter tears. He felt that fate had dealt him a cruel blow, unjustifiably cruel, in return for his moderation.

What could be done to him ? Baron Wunderhausen, who now, as Sonia's husband, lived with the family, suggested handing the man over to the Bolshevik militia. But Nikolai Vasilievich only waved his hand. I think it was the family aspect of the old man's position that penetrated Nikolai Vasilievich to the heart. He sat there at his desk, brooding darkly, while Stanitski, gently, like a cat, felt his way out of the flat.

Fanny Ivanovna sighed conspicuously.

'An optimistic gentleman—Stanitski,' I remarked. 'What a belief in the kindliness of things! What a claim on the favour of Providence!'

'And, as it happens, he is not far wrong in his calculations,' said the Baron with a bitterness which showed that he, as son-in-law, was dissatisfied with the management of the family's finances. 'I call this state of things disgraceful.'

'God have mercy upon us!' whispered Fanny Ivanovna, almost ironically.

'An optimist,' I digressed aloud, 'is a fool, since he can't see what awaits him—disillusionment. But he is wise without knowing it, since, however bad the present, he remains an optimist as to the future, and so his present seems never quite so bad to him as it really is.'

'Say it again,' breathed Nina.

'A fool,' said Nikolai Vasilievich, 'is an optimist. He is optimistic about himself, optimistic about his folly. *I'm* an optimist!'

He stood up, his hands in his trouser pockets, and gazed at the window. Twilight was falling swiftly. Nina, perched up on the sofa, sat silent, her head bent.

'What's the good of being miserable?' I said to her.

'As though I deliberately chose to be miserable!' To console herself, she took an apple.

'Optimists that we are!' sighed Fanny Ivanovna.

'Warranting considerable pessimism,' supplied the Baron.

'It is easier to hope,' said Nikolai Vasilievich, 'and be disappointed, it is easier to hope knowing that one will be disappointed, than not hope at all."

'Why don't the writers—the novelists—why don't they write about this, this real life,' said Fanny Ivanovna, 'this real drama of life, rather than their neat, reasoned, reasonable and—oh! so unconvincing novels?'

'This philosophizing won't help us,' jeered Nikolai Vasilievich mildly. 'We ought to *do* things. I want to *do* things. This moment I am teeming over with energy. I could do and settle things to-day, square up our affairs, and start life afresh.—But——'

The Baron looked at him. 'Well ?'

'But——' His gesture at the window indicated the obstacle. 'What can I do with *this* ? What can anybody do ? All is tumbling, going to ruin. In a month or so all business will stop, works will close down. The rouble will be value-less. There will be *nothing*...'

'Now don't lose courage, Nikolai,' said Fanny Ivanovna hopefully. 'We shall pull through ; somehow we shall ; and then on the other side of the grave we shall be safe.'

'Her most optimistic moment in life !' jeered Nikolai Vasilievich.

'It's a surprising thing what the human soul will stand, Andrei Andreiech,' she said. 'I can venture only this explanation ; it is habit. You see, the cup is ever filled to the brim, but—lo ! the miracle ! the cup expands. No trouble. None !—And here we are.'

'Life gets you,' came from the window ; 'sooner or later it gets you all the same.'

'I don't know what it's for, why, or who wants it. It seems so unnecessary, useless, even silly. And yet I cannot think that it's all in vain. There must be—perhaps a larger pattern somewhere in which all these futilities, these shifting incongruities are somehow reconciled. But shall we know ? Shall we ever know the reason ?'

'Philosophy !' jeered Nikolai Vasilievich mildly.

'Perhaps,' I said, 'when we awaken on the other side of death and ask to be told the reason, they will shrug their shoulders and say, " We don't know. It is beyond us. Do *you* not know ? "—And we shall never know. *Never*...'

'How awfully funnily your mouth moves when you speak,' said Nina, who had been listening to me attentively.

'Frightfully !'

'There is no proof,' said Baron Wunderhausen, 'that death *is* the end. But there is no proof, as yet, that death is *not* the end.'

'So there is no proof of anything?' asked Nikolai Vasilievich.

'No.'

'Thank you,' said Fanny Ivanovna.

The Baron bowed.

Then Nikolai Vasilievich passed into the hall and put his coat on. As it was time for me to go, we went out together. I remember there was something hopeless about that night, a sense of dread about the political and economic chaos, that seemed to harmonize with Nikolai Vasilievich's state of mind. I think it may be that he found a kind of ghastly pleasure in the thought that if he was miserable, if destitution stared him in the face, the whole world also seemed to be tumbling about him into decay and ruin. As we crossed the Palace Square we were challenged by a soldier who had emerged from behind a pile of firewood dumped before the Winter Palace. He stepped forward with fixed bayonet and demanded money, while pointing his bayonet at my breast; he held his finger on the trigger. He was considerably drunk. Neither of us happened to have any money. 'Got any cigarettes, Comrades?' he asked.

Neither of us had cigarettes.

'And I,' explained the drunken soldier, 'go about, you know, letting the guts out of the *bourgouys*.'

'That's right, Comrade,' ventured Nikolai Vasilievich. 'Kill them all, the dirty dogs!'

'I will,' said the soldier cheerily, and stalked off into the night, while we went our way.

Nikolai Vasilievich only shook his head and sighed and shook his head and sighed. He muttered something, but the wind that overtook us carried off his words. I could just catch '—my house—the mines——'

# PART III

INTERVENING IN SIBERIA

# I

CERTAIN fragments of scene and speech come back to me with a peculiar insistence, as I write this third portion of my book. I have no hesitation in setting them down as I do, I think accurately enough, if not word for word. I remember them well because they had impressed me. That is the secret of memory. I have forgotten much, but there are scenes I cannot forget, fragments of speech that still ring in my ear, and I shall remember them always ; at least, till I have finally pinned them to paper.

The Admiral and I, and a few others—interesting types, I can assure you—travelled to Siberia, where we engaged in a series of comic opera attempts to wipe out the Russian revolution. By now, 'Intervention' has been relegated to the shelf of history. But I cannot but remember it, not merely as an adventure in futility, as admittedly it was, but as an ever-shifting, changing sense of being alive. For the experience of love is inseparable from its background. Alone it does not exist. It is a modulation of impressions, an interplay of 'atmospheres,' a quickening of the fibres of that background into throbbing tissues of an elusive, half-apprehended beauty.

It was raining heavily when we arrived in Vladivostok, and the port, as we surveyed it from the boat, looked grey and hopeless, like the Russian situation. A flat had been allotted us, a bare, unfurnished flat in a deserted house standing in a grim and desolate by-street; and there the Admiral made his temporary headquarters. It poured all day long, and it seemed, indeed, as though the rain, playing havoc with the town, would never cease, even as the misery and blundering in Russia would never cease, and that our efforts were not wanted and could do no good.

That night I entertained General Bologoevski at dinner

at the famous restaurant ' Zolotoy Rog '—nicknamed by
British sailors the ' Solitary Dog.' He had travelled with
us all the way from England, seemingly under vague
instructions from some Allied War Office, and had attached
himself to our party of his own accord. As we sat down, the
head waiter came up to us and respectfully informed the
General that by order of the Commander-in-Chief Russian
officers were not admitted into restaurants. The General
protested feebly, stressing his hunger as a reason for
remaining, whereon the head waiter suggested, in an undertone, that the obvious alternative was to remove the
epaulets.

' What! Remove my epaulets! I, a Russian officer?
Never!' he protested.

Whereon a brain-wave struck him. ' I know,' he said,
looking round the restaurant. It was nearly empty. And
instantly he compromised by putting on his mackintosh.
' Now,' said he, ' in my English Burberry they will take me
for an English officer. Ah!' he smiled, and then added his
invariable English phrase : ' It is a damrotten game, you
know.' And, after a momentary contemplation : ' I give
dem h-h-hell!'

I ordered chicken soup. The General talked loosely about
the Siberian situation. About five minutes after I had
ordered soup the waiter returned without being called and
very amiably volunteered the information that the soup
would be served immediately. When, three-quarters of an
hour later, I asked the waiter about the soup, he repeated
' immediately,' but the word now somehow failed to inspire
in us the same confidence. The General talked of the
Siberian situation for about an hour and a quarter, when
we observed that the soup had not been served. I again
called the waiter.

' What about that soup ? ' I asked.

' I am afraid, sir,' said the waiter, ' you will have to wait
a while, for soup is a troublesome thing to prepare
nowadays.'

' How long ? '

' About three-quarters of an hour.'

General Bologoevski then continued about the situation. I gathered that there was a General Horvat who had formed an All-Russia Government, and that there was also a Siberian Government, defying General Horvat on the one hand and the Bolsheviks on the other, and that there were various officer organizations grouped about this or the other government, and some rather inclined to be on their own, all looking forward to a possible intervention by the Allies. After an hour or so had elapsed I interrupted General Bologoevski by observing that the soup had not yet been served, and I called a waiter who was passing and told him to fetch the waiter who had been serving us.

' He has gone to bed,' came the answer, ' and I am on the night shift.'

' Oh ! ' And I inquired about the soup.

' Soup ? ' said the new waiter, evidently disowning all responsibility for his predecessor, and after some hesitation he promised us some soup in about three-quarters of an hour. General Bologoevski then continued about the situation. He spoke for an intolerably long time, stopping only once or twice to inquire about the soup and whether it was coming. The clock in the corner chimed midnight, and then one. I was now devilishly hungry, and the General looked misused and maltreated. I shouted for the waiter, who with eyes closed slumbered in a standing posture in the distant corner of the room. ' What about that soup ? ' I repeated in excited tones when the waiter showed signs of recovering consciousness.

' Soup ? ' he asked. ' Well, you see you can't have soup nowadays. . . unless you choose to wait——'

' *Wait !* ' I said.

' Three-quarters of an hour or so,' he said.

Whereupon the General rose. He rose in a threatening manner. It seemed to me that the General's manner of rising was deliberately remonstrative, a protest undisguised.

'General!' I shouted as he ran across to his hat and sword. 'Come back and have something. A chicken cutlet. General!'

But he was gone. I sat alone at my table and waited for the cutlet. As I looked before me I observed sitting at a distant table a man with a familiar face. I could not believe it. My heart leapt within me. I dashed from my chair.

'Nikolai Vasilievich!'

'Andrei Andreiech!'

'Is it possible? Is it really you?'

Nikolai Vasilievich was kissing me on both cheeks, in confirmation of his identity.

'Well, I never thought that you were here! I never thought that you could be here, Nikolai Vasilievich.'

'I am here,' said Nikolai Vasilievich sadly.

'And who else is here, who else, Nikolai Vasilievich?'

'All,' sighed Nikolai Vasilievich.

'All! How do you mean all?'

'*All.*'

'Fanny Ivanovna here?'

'Yes, she is here.'

'Nina?'

'Yes, she is here.'

'And Pàvel Pàvlovich?'

'Yes, both Pàvel Pàvlovichi are here.'

'And Eberheim?'

'Yes, he is here too . . . they're all here.'

'You don't say so!... And Čečedek?'

'All here—all.'

'And Vera?'

'Yes.'

'And Sonia?...'

'Yes, all—my wife and all.'

'Which wife, Nikolai Vasilievich?'

'How do you mean? I only have one—Magda Nikolaevna.'

' Oh, you haven't married Zina then ? '

' No, but she is here.  They are all here—all her family—
Uncle Kostia—all.'

' How are they all ?  Tell me, Nikolai Vasilievich—the
grandfathers dead, I suppose ? '

' Oh no, both here.  But I don't think—nobody thinks—
they can last very long now, either of them.'

' Oh, they're alive.  That's good——  And so Magda
Nikolaevna is here too—with Čečedek, of course.'

' Yes, and Eisenstein.'

' She has married Čečedek ? '

' No, she has married no one—except me, of course.  But
I expect it won't be very long now till I get a divorce.'

My voice dropped to a confidential whisper.  ' Why are
they all here, Nikolai Vasilievich ? ' I asked.

' Andrei Andreiech, don't ask me.  Why is it that they
followed me here all the way from Petrograd ?  And when
I had to go over to Japan just for a fortnight on a matter of
business—well, they all followed me there—all—every one
of them !—You see, they are, so to speak, economically
dependent on me.  That is why I suppose they follow me
about wherever I go.  We are inseparable—financially.  We
are a chain.  Russia being what she is to-day—disjointed,
with neither railway nor postal communication that you can
rely on, they simply have to be where I am if they are to get
money out of me.  I quite understand their position.  So
they follow me, you see.'

' Nikolai Vasilievich ! '  And I shook him long and
warmly by the hand.

We sat together long into the morning, and Nikolai
Vasilievich complained of his lot.  The mines, it seemed,
were still the chief deterrent to his happiness.  His family, he
said, had decided to leave Petrograd and go east because
their house, which, strictly speaking, belonged to them
no longer, had, since the Bolshevik revolution, been in-
vaded by a host of undesirable people and there was hardly
a room left in the house that they could call their own.

Another reason which prompted them to leave the capital was that the Bolshevik authorities had restricted individuals from drawing on their current accounts in the banks ; and what was more important still, Nikolai Vasilievich had really nothing left in the bank to draw upon. So he had naturally turned to his other source of income—the gold-mines in Siberia. He had poured considerable money into these gold-mines in the past, in the hope that some day they would make him very wealthy. For years and years they had a way of ever being on the eve of making him wealthy, yet always some minor, unforeseen incident occurred which temporarily postponed the realization of his hopes. The gold-mines were about to begin to pay, when war broke out and temporarily affected the output. Then in the war he perceived the opportunity of placing them on a military footing. The governor, a friend of his, had promised to assist him, when unhappily the revolution came and the governor was arrested and dismissed. Kerenski's time was the most trying time of all. For then the miners began to call committee-meetings and talk as to what they would do when they seized the mines ; but they confined their revolutionary schemes to a violent expression as to what they *would* do, in the meantime doing nothing, either in the taking over of the mines or in the working of them. With the Bolshevik revolution things began to move, and the men seized the mines. At first the news was a great shock to Nikolai Vasilievich, for he knew that there were many families dependent on him. Then he perceived that he could actually buy the gold from the men at exactly the same price as it had cost him to produce it. He was much relieved, and for the first time in his life he was actually doing good business.

It was then that they decided to leave Petrograd for Siberia, and his families, dependants and hangers-on natur-ally all followed him. He travelled with Fanny Ivanovna, Sonia, Nina, Baron Wunderhausen, Kniaz, Eberheim and the book-keeper Stanitski. His wife was in the same train, but in a different carriage, and she insisted on having Vera with her, for she was not well, and Čečedek was merely a man. Eisenstein followed her. At times it seemed as if he had lost sight of them ; but he invariably turned up by the next train in every town they halted. Eberheim was a great trouble. He suffered terribly. At several wayside stations they had to take him out and put him into hospital. Sometimes there was no hospital, only a doctor. Sometimes there was no doctor, and Zina's father attended to him as best he could. Eisenstein too was helpful. On more than one occasion Zina's family—the largest family of all—and Magda Nikolaevna's party, had gone on not knowing that Nikolai Vasilievich's party had remained behind ; and Nikolai Vasilievich thought that he would never see them again. But they had discovered his absence and waited for him in the next town along the line, before proceeding farther. The two old grandfathers stood the journey very well on the whole, considering their advanced age and the hardships of the trip. What made it very unpleasant for Nikolai Vasilievich was that the various parties who were financially dependent on him were not on speaking terms with one another. He was besieged with notes requesting private interviews, and there were violent disputes which he was called upon to settle. When at length he had arrived at the headquarters of his gold-mines, he learnt that the Czecho-Slovak troops in their recent offensive against the Bolsheviks had recaptured the mines, shot the miners' leaders, imprisoned many other miners, and then handed the mines back to his manager ; whereon the miners killed the manager and refused to resume work. Mr. Thomson, his consulting-engineer, despairing of the situation, had returned to England. And Nikolai Vasilievich perceived that his recent scheme of purchasing the gold from the men had been completely knocked on the head.

He was now considering another scheme that had been suggested to him by a number of financiers in the Far East, which involved the active co-operation of two influential generals—to organize and dispatch a punitive expedition to the gold-mines in order to compel the miners to restart work. This somewhat complicated scheme had necessitated a trip to Tokio to interest another Russian general who was there in the scheme ; and all the families, no doubt thinking that he was trying to escape from his responsibilities, followed him to Tokio, thus unnecessarily increasing his expenses. He had had great difficulty in finding accommodation for his family in Vladivostok ; but for Fanny Ivanovna, Sonia, Nina, Vera, Baron Wunderhausen and himself he had procured the ground floor of a little house. All the others had also settled down in Vladivostok. And the Baron would, no doubt, find it difficult to evade military service.

'And how are you?' asked Nikolai Vasilievich. 'I wondered if you would be coming with the Admiral. We half expected that you would. Well, what do you think of it?'

'Think of it!' I said. 'Why, we are the men of the hour. You should have seen the deputations, proclamations, speeches, hailing him as the new Lafayette. He said to-day, jokingly, of course, that he would have to work out a time-table for seeing people. Dictators, say, from 7 to 10 ; supreme rulers between 10 and 1; prime ministers could be admitted between 2 and 5. Then till seven he would be free to cabinet ministers of the rank and file. Supreme commanders-in-chief could come from 8 to 1. And so forth, down to common general officers commanding. Yes, it was hardly an exaggeration.'

Nikolai Vasilievich smiled one of his kindly smiles. 'Do you think it will be all right?' he asked.

'Rather!' I replied irrelevantly. 'It's the climax of his career. He has been called upon by four joint deputations representing, I think, four separate All-Russia Governments whose heads conferred on him the title of " Supreme Commander-in-Chief of All the Armed Military and Naval Forces operating on the Territory of Russia," or something of this sort. And he made a speech to them ; said that Foch was wrong and Douglas Haig was wrong, and all those muddle-headed politicians ! The war was to be won on the Eastern Front.'

'I too think it will be won on the Eastern Front,' said Nikolai Vasilievich. 'It ought to, anyhow.'

'Why ? '

' Well, because the Eastern Front has unquestionably the greater resources in mineral wealth. The gold-mines ought to be cleared of the enemy before anything else if you want to win the war.'

'Yes,' I said with an assumed and exaggerated pensiveness, ' that is unquestionably the case.'

We arranged to meet again to-morrow, as we descended arm in arm the shabby flight of steps, and it was decided that Nikolai Vasilievich should call for me and drive me home to see the family.

The rain had ceased. We parted at the cross-roads.

When I turned into my bedroom I beheld the Admiral and a little dark-haired man, aquiline featured, sitting on my bed and talking like two conspirators. The dark-haired little man then rose with the precision common to Russian officers, and shook hands. He was, I learnt afterwards, Admiral Kolchak.

It was very late that night when I fell asleep. I was thinking of my meeting on the morrow with the family, with Nina. I pictured to myself her image as I last remembered it. And, interlacing with these thoughts, there was the thought of the gallant Admiral in the bedroom opposite, tucked away between his heavy blankets, his teeth in a glass of water on the table at his side—no presentable sight !— seeing visions of a Napoleonic ride athwart the great Siberian plain, at the head of his vast new armies marching onward to take their stand on the re-established Eastern Front.

Then in the small hours of the morning he was wakened by the noise of a dog that ran through the half-open door of his bedroom in pursuit of a cat. I heard the Admiral strike a match, then jump out of bed and fumble with his stick under the bed and cupboards and chest of drawers, evidently looking for the animals. I went in to him and offered my services in the chase.

'Can you see the dog?' came the Admiral's sturdy voice from under a cupboard.

'I'm looking for the cat, sir.'

'Cat! Where did *that* come from?'

'I saw it run into your room after a rat.'

'Nonsense!'

'I did, sir, and the dog ran in after the cat.'

We fumbled with our sticks.

'I don't believe there was a rat,' said the Admiral.

'There was, sir. I saw it myself.'

'I don't mind the dog so much. Cats I hate. But I can't stick the rat. Why did you tell me?'

I did not answer this.

'Can't find them, sir,' I said, rising.

'They've gone, I hope,' said the Admiral.

'They've hidden themselves somewhere, I think.'

'Damn them! I shan't be able to sleep all night.'

'Good night, sir.'

The Admiral could not sleep. I heard him get out of bed and fumble with his stick beneath the furniture. I think the uncertainty of the whereabouts of the animals disturbed his peace of mind. Then I heard him creep into bed, and all was still. I could just hear the rain drum against the window-pane; and I thought that by now the cat had probably eaten up the rat.

## II

Nikolai Vasilievich was to call for me after lunch. At lunch there were many guests, and the conversation was necessarily political. I was impatient, for Nikolai Vasilievich might call at any moment; and the entire scheme of 'Intervention ' seemed to me, in my mood of acute expectancy, singularly unimportant. I watched the Admiral who in his serious, deliberate way looked straight into his principal guest's eyes and listened very earnestly and nodded with approval, while the guest, a Russian General, was talking arrant nonsense. In that stiff and martial attitude common to a certain type of Russian officer (who assumes it as it were in proof of grim determination) the guest was saying : ' All these complaints about arrests and executions by the loyal troops—I decline to take them seriously. In the present wavering state of mind of the population you can't guarantee that there won't be people who will complain because the sun shines in the daytime only and not at night as well.'

The Admiral gave an emphatic nod ; and at a glance I could see that he had classed his guest as a ' good fellow.' The Admiral, I may explain, divided the world into two big camps : the humanity that he called ' good fellows,' and the humanity that he called ' rotters '—and there you are ! Simple. (As a matter of fact, he used a substitute for this last word, but I am afraid the original is unprintable.) But while the guest was being engaged by General Bologoevski, a quiet silver-haired British Colonel took the opportunity of telling the Admiral in his quiet silvery manner the conclusion he in his quiet silvery mind had quietly arrived at after interviewing for many months innumerable Russian officers. ' I am afraid,' said he, ' that whenever you come to examine very carefully a Russian officer's scheme for the restoration and salvation of his country, it invariably boils down to giving him a job.'

And at a glance I could see that the Admiral had classed the fellow as a ' rotter.'

I forget the substance of the conversation of that lunch, which stands out in my memory merely on account of its coincidence with the day on which I met the family ; but I remember how a remark of General Bologoevski's, that he understood the Bolshevik commissars never washed, lit up the Admiral's face with ominous glee, and one could guess at sight that he condemned the Bolshevik commissars.

About two o'clock Nikolai Vasilievich called for me. We drove uphill, the driver flogging his two horses with unwarranted zeal. The day was bright, but the roads were muddy from the flood overnight. As we arrived, another cab drove up at the porch, and from it emerged Fanny Ivanovna and Kniaz. Kniaz made an insincere attempt to pay the cab-fare; but when Fanny Ivanovna said 'It's all right, I have some money,' Kniaz said, ' Very well,' and replaced the empty purse in his pocket.

And for the next few minutes the three-roomed lodging of the little house was the scene of a happy reunion.

Nina alone was absent from the household. Fanny Ivanovna was much annoyed and tackled Sonia on the subject.

' How do I know where she is ? ' Sonia remonstrated. Then she smiled and I felt that she knew all right; and then immediately she grew angry, and I felt that after all, perhaps, she did not know.

' We have no means of knowing, Fanny Ivanovna,' said Baron Wunderhausen.

' Pàv'l Pàvlch,' she said, ' please don't annoy me. You annoy me with your inconsequent talk, and I have asked you not to meddle—and to wash your neck.'

' He's like Uncle Kostia ! ' Vera cried. ' Has a bath once a year—whether clean or dirty.' She was pretty, growing prettier.

Baron Wunderhausen only shrugged his shoulders.

Then the door opened and Nina slipped into the room. I was staggered by her looks. To my mind she was irresistible. When she saw me she stopped dead.

' Where have *you* come from ? ' she asked.

I explained confusedly, and a minute later she dismissed me and my arrival as a thing entirely commonplace, and turned to the others.

'Nina,' said Fanny Ivanovna sternly, 'where have you been ? I insist on your telling me.'

'And I won't tell,' said Nina curtly.

'Nina,' I took it up, jokingly but with a sneaking sense of secretive authority resting on our 'engagement' of four years ago, 'where have you been? I too insist on your telling me.'

She looked at me with the expression that comes over people who are about to put out their tongue at you, and said :

'And I won't tell.'

'And how do you find us ? ' Fanny Ivanovna asked. ' Have we grown older ? I think I have grown older. And Nikolai Vasilievich, too. And Kniaz.'

'No,' I lied. And assuredly the lie pleased her.

'And the children are just the same ? '

'The children are just the same,' I agreed. 'A bouquet. Three pretty kittens.'

Vera purred like one.

'But you haven't much room here, have you?' I observed.

'What can we do?' she asked. 'The town is packed with refugees. We can't find anything better.'

' *A la guerre comme à la guerre,*' remarked the Baron.

'Still, it is more comfortable than living in an hotel. Sonia, Nina and Vera sleep here on the sofa and the bed we drag out from the other room. The adjoining room is Nikolai Vasilievich's and mine. The third is Pàv'l Pàvlch's, the Baron's. The others have remained at the hotel—I mean Kniaz and Eberheim. I don't care what Magda Nikolaevna does, but I think she has now found a house. And Uncle Kostia and the rest of them will probably settle at his sister's, the Olenins. Kniaz comes here for his meals and spends the day with us—though lately '—she smiled—' he has been going out hunting.'

'Hunting ! ' I exclaimed, looking at the Prince's well-shaved chin.

Kniaz passed his fingers between his skinny neck and his stiff collar in a nervous gesture and giggled feebly.

' He's bought a gun,' said Nina.

' You should see the gun ! ' Vera cried.

Fanny Ivanovna smiled ; and as we settled down to tea Nikolai Vasilievich chaffed Kniaz in his timid, deferential manner. ' I went out hunting with him once. It's a comedy ! We see a hare. Kniaz pulls the trigger once—misfire. Pulls at it again—misfire. Pulls at it a third time—and the gun misfires for the third time. When he had pulled the trigger a fourth time there was a terrible explosion ; a blaze of fire burst forth from the muzzle ; the butt end hit him violently in the shoulder. And when the smoke had gradually dispersed we saw that the hare had evidently escaped undamaged. His instrument of murder was the only victim ; and there I saw Kniaz looking at his gun : the trigger and most of the front piece had blown off in the concussion. But there he stood, still holding the instrument in his hands, puzzled beyond words.'

Nikolai Vasilievich looked at Kniaz and smiled kindly, as though to make up by it for any pain that his recital may have caused him.

Nina stretched a plate of sweets to me.

I looked at her interrogatively.

' With your tea,' she said.

' There is no sugar,' said Nikolai Vasilievich apologetically.

' I want to speak to you very seriously,' said Baron Wunderhausen, ' about transferring to the English Service.'

' Now that Andrei Andreiech has arrived,' said Fanny Ivanovna gaily, ' we shall be able to get sugar and everything from the English.'

' The English are all right,' said Nikolai Vasilievich. ' I always did have confidence in the English. If the English once begin a job you may be sure they'll see it through. And if the first step is taken and the mining area is liberated, Bolshevism will soon collapse.'

'I want to speak to you about my special qualifications for transferring to the English Service. I was born and educated——'

'Pàv'l Pàvlch,' cried Fanny Ivanovna, 'please don't interrupt. I want you, Andrei Andreiech, to translate an English letter Nikolai Vasilievich has received from his former mining-engineer, Mr. Thomson. Our English is not quite sufficient, though I've understood parts of it.'

I took the letter. Mr. Thomson, writing from an obscure address in Scotland, stated that the after-war conditions prevailing in the west of Europe had frankly disappointed him, and solicited an invitation to be reinstated in his former post as consulting-engineer in Nikolai Vasilievich's gold-mines.

'It's such a pity,' Fanny Ivanovna sighed. 'Mr. Thomson is such a nice man. And now it seems he is so badly off. It must be terrible for his wife and children.'

'Well,' said Nikolai Vasilievich, 'I say this : it's no use Mr. Thomson coming out here *at present*, while the mines are still in Bolshevik hands. And I don't want to hold out false hopes to Mr. Thomson, for one can never quite be sure what may happen in Siberia yet. But between ourselves, I may tell you that now that the English have arrived and—well, that this punitive expedition to the mines has been arranged, we have good reason to feel optimistic.'

'Well, let's hope, let's hope,' said Fanny Ivanovna.

But the three sisters looked as if they didn't care a hang about Mr. Thomson, the English, the mines or anybody else.

'Are you going to the dance ? ' said Nina.

'Which dance ? '

'The Russian one—at the Green School.'

'But it will be Russian dances all the time.'

'Doesn't matter.'

'Russian music, too.'

'We can dance fox-trots to krokoviaks, one-steps to march music, slow waltzes to anything you like. You must come.'

I knew I was going, but I liked to be asked, and I resisted lingeringly, to prolong the pleasure.

Of course I was going. Who could have resisted this sliding side-long look; this shining semicircle of white teeth that revealed itself with each full smile; this lithe, sylphine young body?

The three sisters affected a stationary fox-trot.

The passions were aroused.

'Nikolai Vasilievich! Papa!'

He was dragged, like a resisting malefactor, struggling, to the piano, and made to play his one and only waltz. The Baron claimed Vera. Nina came automatically into my arms. I recaptured some of her familiar fragrance, as we danced between the sofa and round the table, dodging sundry chairs. Sonia stood demurely at the wall, abandoned by her husband in favour of a younger sister, but affecting an unconvincing *moue* of mirth. Then, owing to the shortness and simplicity of the tune, Nikolai Vasilievich's technique broke down.

'I want to talk to you on this very serious question of transferring to the English Service.' The Baron had come up to me again. And I resorted to the classic answer of doubting whether there was 'any vacancy.'

'It doesn't matter *where*,' he said. 'In Persia, or perhaps in Mesopotamia. I can't serve here any longer.'

We sat silent in the heated room of the little wooden house creaking in the wind, and I felt lost and hidden amid all this sun and fir and solitude around us. Nikolai Vasilievich drank his tea and wondered if the Bolsheviks would hand him back his house and money at the bank, and if the Czechs, as obviously they ought, would compensate him for his loss on the gold-mines. He had great hopes, he said, of the punitive expedition; but there was one aspect—a moral one—that disturbed him greatly. He wondered whether the punitive expedition would turn out to be quite honest and would not do him out of his interests in the gold-mines altogether.

Afterwards he came up to me and said in a weary undertone : ' You know, it will be very dull to-night—nothing but Russian dance music. Honestly, it would only spoil your evening if you went.'

' Don't take any notice of him,' cried the three sisters simultaneously. ' It will be very jolly. He's only thinking of himself.'

' Nikolai ! ' cried Fanny Ivanovna. ' What nonsense ! You've already promised me to come. You're their father and it's your duty to take your children out. I refuse to go alone with them.'

As I entered the brilliantly illuminated ball-room, the three sisters, each claimed by an Allied officer, were fox-trotting, in defiance of the congregation. Nikolai Vasilievich wearing a dinner-jacket, looked very angry, very lonely and very bored ; and Fanny Ivanovna looked ominously triumphant.

' Poor Nikolai Vasilievich ! ' I said when Fanny Ivanovna and I were alone. ' That dinner-jacket of his looks miserable and frightened as though it felt the outrage of being dragged into this mock festivity. It seems to say : " What have I done ? " '

' Doesn't matter. He is better where he is.

' He would only be with that girl of his if I had not insisted on his coming with us,' she added by way of after-thought.

' Zina ? '

' *Ach !* Andrei Andreiech ! It makes me so ill, so angry to think of it.'

Then Nikolai Vasilievich, ludicrously festive, strolled up to us.

' Well,' he muttered, yawning into his white-cuffed hand.

' Jolly dance,' I said.

' For those who dance,' he retorted in a voice as though I had foully and grievously betrayed him.

Then the music ceased abruptly. The three sisters, scantily and deliciously attired, glided up, and were met with an involuntary critical examination from the eyes of Fanny Ivanovna, who effected a few, to all appearance needless, pulls at their evening-gowns.

' I could hardly recognize Nina with her hair like this,' I remarked aloud.

With sylphine litheness, she slid between me and Baron Wunderhausen to the drawing-room.

' Really, I don't like the way you've done your hair,' I said. ' There's nothing at the front.'

Instantly she vanished to the dressing-room ; and in her absence the Baron tackled me again about a billet in Persia or Mesopotamia. I expressed a mild surprise. ' Have we not come here to help the Russian national cause ? ' I asked. ' Is that then of no interest to you ? '

' You know,' he said nonchalantly, ' nothing will come of it.'

' Why ? '

' The Czechs are such awful swine. They're all Bolsheviks.'

And then added, ' And the Americans, too, are Bolsheviks. President Wilson. Nothing will come of it all.'

And, involuntarily, the conversation at lunch surged back to my mind. I thought this equalled it in point of sheer ' constructive statesmanship.' And then Nina, now in her original coiffure, returned.

We sat under dusty imitation palm-trees, my sleeve every now and then touching her shapely naked girlish arms ; till Nikolai Vasilievich came up and gave us supper, insisting on paying for it all himself. I thought of the poor, long-suffering mines who would eventually have to square all this, as I surveyed the debris on the tablecloth, while Nikolai Vasilievich paid the waiter.

When the music, after the due interval, broke out into a resounding waltz, we all flocked back into the ball-room.

General Bologoevski, who had turned up at the eleventh hour, stood at my side, and we admired Nina, who now fulfilled a carelessly contrived engagement. ' What eyes ! What calves ! What ankles ! ' he was saying. ' Look here, why in heaven don't you marry her ? '

Driving through the dark and muddy streets, I sat on the folding seat ; the car was packed with members of the family. Tucked away in the corner opposite, like a purring kitten, was Nina. We began to part provisionally at their gate ; but they asked me to come in. We had cold ham and tinned salmon and tea with sweets. There was a certain subdued agitation about my presence in the household at this hour, and once I heard Fanny Ivanovna's shrill voice from the adjoining room explain excitedly to Sonia : ' You needn't drag the bed into the drawing-room till Andrei Andreiech is gone.'

I had been *going* for an hour or so. We had said ' good night ' innumerable times. Nina clung to me whimsically, ignoring Nikolai Vasilievich's desire to be rid of me. They all came out into the tiny hall and added to the difficulty of my withdrawal. Nina fastened my great sheepskin overcoat, which appealed to her by reason of its many straps. I was to come again to-morrow night to supper, and the day after, and every, every day...

### III

My tangled memories of Siberia come to me to-day largely as a string of dances, dinners, concerts, garden-parties, modulated by the atmosphere of weather and the seasons of the year, with the gathering clouds of the political situation looming always in the background. And I remember, in particular, the Admiral's first *thé dansant*. As he ran through my provisional list of guests he frowned and growled a little. ' What are all these women ? ' he asked.

'You should see them, Admiral,' smiled General Bologoevski.

'Good-looking?'

The General kissed his finger-tips.

'And who is Fanny Ivanovna?'

'A German.'

A shadow came across his face. 'I'm damned if I want any Huns in my house,' he growled; but gave in grudgingly.

Through inadvertence on somebody's part, the officers of the U.S. Flagship arrived half an hour before time—an incident which taxed my capacity for consuming liquor to the utmost pitch. They had also overdone their kindness by sending us two jazz bands instead of one, with the result that their almost simultaneous employment in the two adjoining rooms reserved for dancing proved an experience unsatisfactory to the ear. As the Hawaiian string-band flowed and quivered in a languid, plaintive waltz, the adjoining brass-band fairly knocked sparks out of it by bursting into an intoxicating one-step.

Some two hours earlier I had met Vera in the street. She had been to see their dressmaker about the frock in which now, radiant but bashful, she appeared. Almost immediately, the family was followed by the Zina-Uncle Kostia wing, and by Magda Nikolaevna and Čečedek. But they would not speak to one another. Nikolai Vasilievich had been to see me in the morning about bringing Zina; and now he tried to dance with her. But both were awkward and bashful, and the experiment proved unsatisfactory; while Fanny Ivanovna looked on at them sarcastically. Nina whispered to me as we danced: 'After them! Go after them!' her triangular, fur-bordered hat bobbing up into my face in the excitement. And as we overtook them: 'Oh, my God!'

Stepping like a duck, Zina would not turn unless warned beforehand, and even then only half the circle; and Nikolai Vasilievich, exasperated by his futile efforts, asked impatiently: 'Are you dancing in goloshes? Have you rubber soles on your shoes? Or what *is* it?'

They gave it up at last and stood by the wall, in everybody's way, shamefaced and pitiful; and Zina looked as though she regretted her insistence on coming to this dance.

' Will you dance?' I said.

' I've never danced before,' said she. ' But I don't mind trying.' She looked up at her lover. Evidently their experiment did not count. Nikolai Vasilievich smiled feebly.

And, as a preliminary, she stepped on my toe.

My next dance was with Magda Nikolaevna, a beautiful woman enough, but so delicate and with such an elaborate concoction of accessories by way of dress that the chief sensation yielded from the dance with her was one of infinite precaution.

As a *pièce de résistance*, I danced with a little niece of Uncle Kostia, Olya Olenin. She was stout and round, like a football, and we banged into people and against walls carelessly and with the harmlessness of a football.

' To-day I have grown ten years older,' confided Nikolai Vasilievich, as I came up to him. ' I shall not forget it.'

' You take it much too seriously.'

' I blame myself for being such a fool as to have listened to her. I didn't want to come.'

' Nikolai Vasilievich, really!'

' Oh, please don't take it that way. It was charming of you to ask us. I like your Admiral—and that other officer, his assistant, who says " Splendid! Splendid!"'

' Sir Hugo,' I supplied.

Then Uncle Kostia, spectacled, and with the air of a profound philosopher taking stock of his impressions, joined us. ' I've been talking to your Admiral,' he said.

' Well?'

' Fine-looking man. Combines the manner of Napoleon I with the mind, I think, of Napoleon III. Wants to get to Moscow. But what he'll do when he gets there (if he gets there), curiously enough doesn't seem to have occurred to him ! The simplicity of the scheme is touching. All right, let's assume he gets there and plants a constitutional Russian government and retains an Allied army to support it. Will he keep the Allied troops there indefinitely ? And when at last they go, what's to prevent the government from collapsing like a pack of cards at the hands of a population inevitably resentful of foreign interference ? Then there's your country. You think your country will support you. But it will be divided.'

'I disagree,' said Nikolai Vasilievich. ' I'd much rather, for example, the gold-mining area was occupied by English troops, or even by the Japanese, than by the Russians. I know what I am talking about. I am a typical Russian myself. There are honest men in Russia, and there are clever men in Russia ; but there are no honest clever men in Russia. And if there are, they're probably heavy drinkers.'

Uncle Kostia ' pooh-poohed ' this sweeping charge ; but Nikolai Vasilievich continued :

' To take my book-keeper Stantiski. Andrei Andreiech knows him. Dishonest as you make them. And still I am obliged to keep him on. Why ? Because if I took an honest man he would make such a hash of all the books that I wouldn't know where I was at all.'

' But do you know where you are with a dishonest book-keeper, Nikolai Vasilievich ? ' said Uncle Kostia with that keen spasmodic interest that highly abstract men have of taking, periodically, in practical affairs, almost as a relief from themselves. ' I am a man of letters, no business man in any sense ; still it would seem to me——'

' To be candid,' said the other, ' it doesn't matter much either way just now. Till we can get the gold-mines back there is no doing any business. I get money in advance occasionally. He sees to the paying of the interest, which is paid out of the same money, and puts it down in the books. For the present that is all.'

' Hm !—Still, I should do something about that,' said

Uncle Kostia, ' if I may presume to give advice in these matters.'

' When we get the gold-mines there will be time enough to act,' Nikolai Vasilievich answered somewhat gruffly. ' I only mentioned it as an illustration of the political situation we have to contend with. The foreigners here must laugh at our methods ! '

' Why ? They're only muddling up our issues.'

' The idea,' I attempted to amend Uncle Kostia's proposition, ' is that the Allied troops should help to raise and train Russian *cadres* and so lay the foundation for a new Russian Army which, in its turn, would make it possible to rebuild the State. It's not an invasion by foreign troops. You may rest your mind in peace on that point.'

' Oh !—Oh !—If that's the idea,' said Uncle Kostia in augmented tones, ' then I am doubly alarmed ; for I can guess the elements which will form the backbone of this new White Russian Army—monarchists altogether too brainless to realize that theirs is a lost cause.'

' Most of them, I think, would favour a Constitutional Monarchy,' proffered Nikolai Vasilievich.

' A constitutional monarchy in Russia,' retorted Uncle Kostia, ' would invariably be more monarchical than constitutional.'

' Anyhow,' I said, ' do have a drink.'

I could see Sir Hugo's ruddy, weather-beaten face, as he served Fanny Ivanovna with her ice-cream ; and as I came up to her I overheard her say to him in German : ' I think the Bolsheviks are bound to be beaten soon because it is impossible to do any trade while they are in power.'

' Splendid ! ' said Sir Hugo somewhat inconsequently. ' Splendid ! '

' We simply can't recover our mines, and Nikolai Vasilievich——'

She stopped.

She danced heavily ; and as I turned her each time, revolved a few times of her own momentum. She sought to direct me by sheer strength of will. 'Who is steering, Fanny Ivanovna? You or me?' I asked in exasperation.

'I am sorry, Andrei Andreiech,' she answered. 'I do it unintentionally.'

The Baron asked me for the third time about Persia or Mesopotamia; but the Admiral's approach frightened him away.

We watched Kniaz, who was shaking hands cordially with everybody as he took his leave. 'That Kniaz of yours looks as if one day he'd been unspeakably astonished—and remained so ever since.'

'Look at General Bologoevski, sir, dancing with that painted woman.'

The Admiral's face drew out and darkened. 'That man,' said he, 'is the *biggest* fool in the Russian Army.' He pondered. 'The Russian men are no damned good. But the women are splendid! What about that Czech concert to-night? You can bring your women if you like into the box. Don't want the men. Ha! ha! ha! Look at old Hugo talking to the young girls!'

'I'll ask the three sisters.'

'Those three there sitting on the window-sill?'

'Yes.—And Fanny Ivanovna,' I added.

'All right. Let's have the Hun.

'Well, Nikolai Vasilievich,' he turned to his guest. 'I hear you know English very well. Where have you picked it up?'

'No, no,' blushed Nikolai Vasilievich; and said in Russian, 'your English spelling is so difficult. In English you spell a word "London" and pronounce it "Birmingham."'

'Ha! ha! ha! ha!' laughed the Admiral loudly, but with dignity; and then asked, 'Are you comfortable in Vladivostok? Can you get all the food you want for your family? I hope you will tell me if there is anything I can do?'

'I am very grateful,' bowed the Russian.

' Now mind you don't forget to ask.'

Nikolai Vasilievich, as things went, did not forget ; nor did he wait to be asked twice. On the spot he said that he understood the Admiral was shortly travelling by special train up-country, and all he, Nikolai Vasilievich, requested was one modest coupé in that special train, as it was urgent that he should see a certain Russian general at Omsk, relative to the forthcoming punitive expedition to his gold-mines.

The Admiral returned the classic answer : ' I'll see what I can do.'

' Will you kindly introd*oo*ce me to the young lady yonder ? ' said a very smart, stiff-collared U.S. naval officer. He looked in the direction of the window-sill.

' Which one ? '

The next moment he was dancing with Nina.

' Who's that officer ? ' asked General Bologoevski.

' Holdcroft.'

' What eyes ! What calves ! What ankles ! ' he sighed again. ' Look here, really, why in the world don't you marry her ? '

' And now,' I said, ' it's my turn,' as the waltz subsided on the last three beats.

' *Tell me*,' whined Nigger voices, ' *why nights are lonesome*,' and the cymbals beat the pulse ; ' *tell me why days are blue . . .*' And we moved rhythmically to the incantation, stooping, jerking gently, swaying smoothly, like plants in the water. When the song ceased it was immediately encored. And when the bands went, a handful of us, those who had enjoyed it most, lingered for a while. I and Nina, the Baron and his painted lady, Vera and Holdcroft, danced to the husky gramophone ; and Sonia sat on the window-sill and stared at Holdcroft with unmitigated admiration.

And in the evening I called for them in our car and took them to the concert. We arrived a little late because at a point in the journey our progress had been impeded by a

car that blocked the road. Inside was a drunken gentleman
who was being urged by the chauffeur to pay his fare.
' Don't want to pay,' the gentleman responded.

' Then get out ! '

' Don't want to get out.'

' Get out, *you*——'

' Who're you talking to ? ' came from within. ' Don't
you know I'm an officer ? '

' Officer. There's a lot of you here, we know your kind.
—Get out ! '

' Don't want to get out.'

' Then kindly pay your fare.'

' Don't want to pay.'

At length our chauffeur succeeded in disentangling our
car. ' I'm always so frightened for the children. Awful
language these drunkards use,' said Fanny Ivanovna.

The theatre, as we entered the box, was a gallery of
distinguished generals, admirals and Allied high com-
missioners ; and the orchestra was sending forth the
plaintive strains of the familiar Clozecho-Svak marching
song.

I sat next to Nina, and the Admiral was in the other
corner, half screened from the public view by the dusty
curtain. To the great delight of Sonia and Fanny Ivanovna,
there was the Overture to *Tannhäuser* ; and as the initial
pilgrims' chorus was being repeated in its last resort, the
conductor urging the executants to ever greater efforts,
and the trombones blazed away their utmost perturbation, a
chuckle of glee and satisfaction spread over the Admiral's
fine-set face. ' There's more discipline in an orchestra like
this,' said he, ' than in a battalion of Marines,' and clapped
his hands uproariously.

The concert over, the Admiral dispatched me first in his
car with the family and waited for me to return for him.
Driving home through the warm and starry night,
Fanny Ivanovna praised the immaculate politeness of
Sir Hugo ; but added afterwards, ' He's frightfully

nervous, and keeps fiddling with something or other all the time.'

'And keeps saying " Splendid ! Splendid ! " ' added Nina.

'There's something curious about his mind, too,' she said.

'Ah ! you've discovered that ! ' I laughed. ' It's a grasp of the inessential, a passion for detail and exactitude unexcelled in creation. You don't know him. To-day, for instance, I met him on the landing, before lunch. " Hello ! " he said. " Full of work ? " Now it had seemed to me that he said " Full of drink ? " and naturally enough I said, " No, not at this hour, sir." " At what hour do you start, pray ? " he began, and thinking he was talking about cocktails, I said, " Oh, just before dinner." " Hm ! " he said. " Just before dinner. I shall have to look into that." " I'm sorry, sir," I said, " I think I must have heard you wrong. Do you mind telling me again what you said ? " " Hm ! " he said, " I've been talking to you on this landing for the last three minutes on the basis of my original inquiry, and you now ask me what it was I said. I said—I think these were the exact words I used—I said : ' Hello ! ' I said. ' Full of work ? ' " " Full of work ? " I cried, " and I thought you said ' Full of drink.' " " Full of drink," he said, " full of drink indeed. Good morning to you ! " And he went his way.'

The car had pulled up.

' Good night, Andrei Andreiech, and thank you very, very much.'

' Good night,' smiled the three sisters.

The Admiral was bucked as we drove home. I knew that he was fond of young girls. On the other hand, he liked mature women. He praised the girls. I breathed to him that they had praised him.

The Admiral smiled one of his most adorable smiles.

' Fanny Ivanovna,' I said, ' was struck by your appearance.'

The gallant Admiral blushed like a girl.

' There is something in having an appearance,' he said at last.

He looked out into the dark and silent night. Some minutes later he said, with conviction, ' She's a good woman, that Fanny Ivanovna.'

' Russian women are so much more interesting and fascinating,' I babbled, ' than other women.'

' Yes,' he agreed. ' But she's a Boche.'

' Unfortunately,' I sighed.

The Admiral yawned. ' Never mind,' he said. ' I don't mind the Germans. What I can't stick are the dirty Bolsheviks.'

' Russian girls,' I continued, ' are far more interesting and clever than other girls.'

' All girls,' the Admiral replied, ' are stupid.'


IV

Much of my experiences must now appear in the nature of a farce. This is not my fault. A good deal of life is a hilarious farce, and yet, as in the case of the affiliation of Nikolai Vasilievich's family, it all comes about in the proper constitutional way, through a string of human motives. For a week or so Nikolai Vasilievich kept on applying to the Admiral for a coupé in his train to Omsk, in the teeth of implacable refusals. Then, after much opposition from the Admiral, and a passionate, though somewhat vague attempt on the part of Nikolai Vasilievich to identify his personal misfortunes with that of ' honest ' Russia, and the doings of the Czechs, the miners, and the punitive expedition whose disinterestedness he had begun to doubt, with that of international Bolshevism, this was conceded. But on hearing of this step, Fanny Ivanovna at once concluded that Nikolai Vasilievich was trying to escape from her—a suspicion she always entertained—and she immediately applied to see the

Admiral in person and asked for two additional coupés, to accommodate her and the three sisters. The Admiral was a sailor and a gentleman. He promised her two coupés.

I forget which wing of the family was the next to apply. I remember that every day that week our waiting-room was crowded with petitioners. The Admiral said No. He found himself saying No innumerable times each day. Now it is an intrinsic part of the Russian character that it does not accept No for No. It is constitutionally incapable of doing so. Its institutions are all a negation of that principle. And what is more, it refuses to confine that fact to within the Russian border. It regards it in the light of world-wide application, assuming that it is indeed nothing less than human nature.

The Admiral still said No. He held that it was not human nature but just Russian nature, and as an illustration of his point he meant to show that when an Englishman says No he does mean No. But none of them would understand the Admiral's interpretation of No. They had all grown up with the idea that No meant Yes after an adequate amount of pressure and insistence. The pressure was of various kinds, according to the age, sex and nature of the applicant. There were tears, entreaties. There were questions, such as the ' object ' of the Allies in Siberia, since they monopolized the best trains and refused to help the Russians in their primary needs. There were direct questions which it was thought must needs shatter the impregnability of the Admiral's No, such as, for instance : Did the Admiral wish to starve them, as he evidently did, by cutting them adrift from Nikolai Vasilievich, the bread-winner ?

The Admiral still said that No was No, and would they please understand it ? They all replied that No was not the point, the point being : *What were they to do without Nikolai Vasilievich?* Whereon the Admiral replied that when he said a thing he meant it, this being the sterling value of British character. But they persisted all the same, treating him as if he were just human like the rest of them. Then the

Admiral became a little angry. It annoyed him that they
should fail to understand the primary fact that an Englishman was not a Russian and that hence any laxity that held
good in Russian character did not hold good in that of a
native of the British Isles. But the Russians hammered on
in spite of all; till the Admiral was heartily amused that
they should indeed know no better than to think that he
would give in just because they persisted, for the ignorance
of human nature that, he thought, such a belief implied—
a quaint and childish ignorance—began to fascinate him. He
looked at them and looked at them again, as they poured
forth their woes—and marvelled. Indeed, their touching
innocence fascinated him so much that finally he felt he
wanted to humour them, as one is inclined to humour quaint,
unreasonable children who know no better. And it was by
way of humouring them that the Admiral gave way. No
(for once only) was to mean Yes. They thanked him cordially. He sighed and wiped his forehead with his handkerchief. The Russian character had won the day.

That night we started on our trip along the great, now
pitiably disorganized Siberian track. It was a lovely night
in late autumn. The Admiral's special train had been
brought over on the main line ; and the General and I, both
somewhat under the influence of liquor, walked arm in arm
up and down the platform ; and the General, in an overflow
of feeling, spoke piteously of his ruined soul, his wasted life,
and how he felt, and what he felt, and why he felt it. The
Admiral and Sir Hugo had already settled down in the
drawing-room of the coach, and were drinking. As the train
moved, we too stepped into the carriage and threw ourselves back on our cushions ; and the General's hand
stretched for the bottle. But I lay back musingly in the dark
carriage, thinking of all things and none in particular, in that
agreeable half-conscious way that is known to precede
slumber, as the train rattled on its way to Omsk.

Two carriages behind us was Nikolai Vasilievico with a
substantial proportion of his family, all bound for Omsk.

When I closed my eyes I could see Nina, and my drowsy thoughts would linger : ' She is *à moi* ... Tucked away in that compartment with her sisters... *A moi*... Now they were undressing for the night... *A moi*... At a handstretch. Always there. But there was no hurry. Oh life . . . leisurely life...! '

I was wakened by the General, and we went and joined the Admiral and Sir Hugo. It seemed that they were both what is known as ' lit up.'

' You're drunk,' the Admiral greeted me.

' And so are you,' I said.

' I know I am, damn you ! '

And we were all very jolly and sang ' *Stenka Razin*,' the Russian robber song, while the train rattled westward. And the General's eyes were moist with tears : he was happy in his melancholy. And, tearfully emotional, he crept to the Admiral, and clinging to his neck tried to kiss him.

' Go away ! ' cried the Admiral in the manner of an innocent young girl about to be accosted ; and then in a more manly tone :

' Damn your eyes ! '

And then the General leaned back with that exaggerated leisure peculiar to his condition, and sang a Russian gipsy song. He spoke of the good old pre-war days. He sighed, sighed deeply. Now everything seemed to have gone wrong, no doubt because his wife who ran him was not here to look after him. But he expected her to come and then all would be well. If he was in a muddle, if he was in debt, as he invariably was, he merely turned to his creditors and said, ' I don't understand all this. Wait till my wife arrives. It's a damrotten game, you know, without my wife. My wife she is a clever woman. She will put it all right with you. My wife she is a dragoon.'

In the night the train stopped at a wayside station and seemed as though it would never start again. The Admiral then sent out the General to find out what was the matter, and Sir Hugo, who attributed the cause to ' bad staff work,' proffered the suggestion of ' negotiating ' with the station-master. But the General said he thought the station-master was a most ' damrotten fellow,' in the case of which type he usually relied on ' elemental ' measures. Accordingly he drew out his pistol and threatened to shoot the station-master like a dog unless he cleared the line immediately. The station-master, used to these methods, took no heed of the warning, but said that he would lodge a vigorous protest through the usual channels. Whereon the General replaced the pistol in his pouch, remarking that life was a ' damrotten game.'

What a trip !

In the morning I observed the Admiral talking to Fanny Ivanovna in his deliberate manner, looking into her eyes. And the impression I received was that the Admiral thought Fanny Ivanovna was a ' good fellow.' But the three sisters, bashful though they were when he spoke to them in English, had somehow overlooked him ; though Nina once remarked, ' How awfully funnily his mouth protrudes when he looks at you so seriously. I feel so shy because I feel *he* does.'

' Now with all this English influence behind him Nikolai Vasilievich ought to be able to find out something definite about his mines at Omsk,' Fanny Ivanovna confided to me. ' And there is no doubt this time we're travelling in comfort. The children are so pleased. You know, they are so childish. Any change like this amuses them.' And then, in a lowered voice : ' Anything like that—love—I assure you, they know absolutely nothing about. They're such children ! '

' But Sonia's married ! ' I remonstrated.

' *Ach !* how that angers me ! And to whom, to *whom* ! He can't even wash his neck. It's all that mother ! '

And so we covered verst after verst, as our luxurious train, freshly painted, beautifully furnished, admirably kept, rushed through a stricken land of misery. On our choice engines we moved like lightning, or perchance stood long hours at lonely wayside stations, the glamour of innumerable electric lights within our carriages presenting to a community of half-starving refugees the gloating picture of the Admiral and his ' staff ' at dinner.

And so we arrived at Lake Baikal, that crystal sea imprisoned in a frame of snow-capped mountains. We stopped our train and lingered on the rocks, drank in the harmony of a strange light, glassy water, snow, fir, and perfect quietude ; and when at last we said good-bye to Lake Baikal, that proudest of lakes, a gale fearful and furious had blown in upon this serenity of beauty and lashed huge waves in the inky blackness of the night.

On went the train, rushing and swaying through the windy space of the fields.

What a trip ! How we argued and wrangled the long journey through ! Sometimes we would almost come to blows ; for the ordinary Russian does not argue : he shouts, and his opponent, to score his point, shouts louder and quicker. The Russian General combined intellectual vagueness with an emotional temperament ; and, contriving to identify his country with his class, he discovered that his country had been grievously insulted by me. All was over between us. He would never speak to me again.

But that evening, after dinner, we sat together over a bottle of whisky, and the General became emotional. ' You are young and foolish,' he said, ' and you probably don't know what you are talking about. I don't. But you love Russia. Tell me you love Russia ; don't you ? We both love Russia. She's been degraded and trampled on ; but she is a fine country. She will arise. She must arise. And we both love Russia.' He sobbed. ' Tell me you love Russia. Tell me you love her. We Russians are lazy, drunken, good-for-nothing swine ; but we are good people, aren't we ? It's a holy land. It's a holy people. Look at her.' He gazed out of the window.

I rose and stood by him, and we looked at Russia, whirling past. Then I left him. When I returned, the General was still lying on the sofa, but his melancholy had vanished and he was spitting at the ceiling, probably for want of anything better to do.

On we went. Two days before we had left Irkutsk. The train rushed and roared and rattled. It was a weather that breeds pessimists. I stood looking out upon the steppes, these immense, monotonous Siberian plains, dull and melancholy in the rain, when Zina came to me and said her mother wished to see me privately. As I entered her coupé the old lady was drinking tea. She bade me sit down.

' It's about Uncle Kostia,' she began. She sighed, and there was a prolonged pause. ' Cleverness ! Wisdom !——Oh, I don't know, Andrei Andreiech. God in heaven knows '—she crossed herself—' that we are groping in the dark and we none of us know what we are about or what's what, and I am an old ignorant, sinful woman. But if you ask me, Andrei Andreiech, I'd just as soon have a fool as a wise man. Take Uncle Kostia. Such a clever man—and what's the good of it ? I am stupid, dotty in my old age, but really I don't see where all his cleverness is leading to. And I say it is time he did something and gave up living upon others. Zina tells me she can't keep on asking Nikolai Vasilievich for money, and I really do think it is time Uncle Kostia began to work—and published something. I thought perhaps you could get the Admiral to place him on some paper—propaganda of some sort. It isn't that one is sorry to keep Uncle Kostia. He is clever, they all say. Heaven knows he has lived on his brother long enough, and one was never sorry to give him all he wanted since the man is clever, you understand, and writes. But now there is nothing to give—since there *is* nothing, you see ? I don't want to appear obdurate or unfeeling ; but I thought perhaps you could talk it over with Uncle Kostia. I know he likes you and he might listen to you.'

I went, promising to do what I could.

When I knocked at the door of Uncle Kostia's coupé it was late in the afternoon. The train rushed, and the dreary monotonous steppes receded, whirling past. Twilight was falling within and without. The candles had not yet been lit. Then the door of the coupé was pulled open and revealed Uncle Kostia sitting on the sofa, laboriously rubbing his eyes. I inquired if I had disturbed him. He assured me that I had not. He sprinkled some eau-de-Cologne on his hands and rubbed his face—a substitute for washing—then made room for me on the sofa, and rubbing his eyes with his fists he yawned widely and looked at the window. The melancholy of the Siberian plain must have communicated itself to both of us. For a time we sat in silence, contemplating the unspeakable disorder of the coupé. I was about to frame an adequate sentence to open conversation when he preceded me.

' There ! ' he said, and struck his forehead with his palm. ' And I am called a clever man. Andrei Andreiech, I have been thinking. I have been thinking a good deal these last days.' He stopped abruptly.

' What have you been thinking about, Uncle Kostia ? ' I asked.

' That's just the trouble,' he said, ' I can't tell you.'

I waited.

' I don't know myself,' he explained.

I still waited.

' I have been thinking of this and that and the other, in fact, of one thing and another—precious but elusive thoughts, Andrei Andreiech. Beautiful emotions. A kaleidoscope of the most subtle colours, if I may so express myself. And, Andrei Andreiech, it has taught me a great truth. It has taught me the futility of writing.'

' But now really, Uncle Kostia,' I remonstrated.

' Don't interrupt me,' said Uncle Kostia. ' It is a truth that only ten per cent, if that, of the substance of our thoughts and feelings can be transferred on paper. It can't be done, Andrei Andreiech—and that's all there is to it.

' And when I think what a fool I have been, writing all

these years, toiling, slaving at a desk like a clerk—when I ought to have been thinking, only thinking.'

' But, Uncle Kostia——' I began.

' Andrei Andreiech, it's no use. How can I *write* down what I think? The subtlety, the privacy, the exquisite intimacy, the thousand and one inexplicable impulses that prompt and make up thought and stir emotion—Andrei Andreiech, how can I? Think! how can I? Oh, you are hopeless—hopeless!—To-day I have been thinking. It will seem nothing to you if I tell you ; it will seem nothing to me if I tell it ; but, believe me, it was something infinitely deep, infinitely complex, infinitely beautiful just when I thought of it—without the labour of exertion.'

' What was it, Uncle Kostia ? ' I inquired.

' It was vague,' he said evasively.

' Oh, come, Uncle Kostia ? '

' How can I tell ? I know too much.'

I was aware of the unpleasant shrinking of ideas when set down on paper. So I persisted :

' Come on, Uncle Kostia ! out with it ! '

' Well,' said Uncle Kostia, and his face became that of a mystic. ' I thought, for instance—I wonder if you will understand me ?—I thought : *Where* are we all going ? '

' Hm,' I said significantly.

' I thought : *Why* are we all moving ? '

' You have not far to seek for motives. I presume there are motives in each case.'

' Motives ! ' he cried. ' That is the very point. There are no motives. The motives are naught. It is the consequences. *Where* are we going ? *Why* are we going ? Look : we are moving. *Going* somewhere. *Doing* something. The train rushes through Siberia. The wheels are moving. The engine-drivers are adding fuel to the engines. Why ? Why are we here ? What are we doing in Siberia ? Where are we heading for ? Something. Somewhere. But *what* ? *Where* ? *Why* ? '

I think I must have misunderstood Uncle Kostia's subtle thoughts. Or was it that my commission was continually in my mind ? But I asked him :

' Is it that you are doomed by your sense of inutility, Uncle Kostia ? '

His eyes flashed. He spoke impatiently : ' *My* inutility ! *Your* inutility ! What the devil does it matter *whose* inutility ? Is your Admiral very *utile*, may I ask ? What I was saying was that we all behaved as if we were actually *doing* things, boarding this Trans-Siberian Express as if in order to *do* something at the end of the journey, while actually the journey is in excess of anything we are likely to achieve.'

But I thought I would keep him to the point, that is to say, *my* point. ' Then would you rather not travel in this train, Uncle Kostia ? '

An anxious look came into his eyes.

' Why ? I like travelling in this train. I am comfortable.'

' But the futility of it ? '

' Oh ! ' groaned Uncle Kostia at my stupidity. ' Can't you understand that it is the very fact of this physical futility that inflates me with a sense of spiritual importance ? '

I looked at him with a blank expression.

' When I am at home—I mean anywhere at a standstill— I am wretched intolerably. I write and I think——' He stopped.

' What ? '

' *What* am I writing for : what on earth am I thinking for ? '

' So you have doubts ? '

' Yes, at moments I am seized by misgivings : what is it all for ? I ask.'

' I see.'

' Now it is different. We are moving, apparently *doing* something, *going* somewhere. One has a sense of accomplishing something. I lie here in my coupé and I think : It is good. At last I am doing something. Living, not recording. Living ! Living ! I look out of the window, and my heart

cries out : Life ! Life ! and so living, living vividly, I lapse
into my accustomed sphere of meditation, and then before
I know exactly where I am I begin to meditate : Where are
we all going to ? Isn't our journey the kernel of absurdity ?
And so, by contrast, as it were, I gain a sense of the importance of meditation.—That is how we deceive ourselves,
Andrei Andreiech.'

' And you can do it in spite of being conscious of the
deception involved ? '

' I have been unconscious of it,' he said, ' until you
forced me into introspection.'

Then, after a pause, I was tickled into inquiring :

' Why don't you—er—publish some of it, eh, Uncle
Kostia ? '

Uncle Kostia grabbed his beard into his fist and looked
at me with pity rather than with scorn and made a movement
as if he was going to spit out of sheer disgust, but evidently
thought better of it. ' You have a front of brass,' he said.
' I cannot penetrate it.'

' Look here, Uncle Kostia,' I cried impatiently, ' you
must be reasonable and think of poor Nikolai Vasilievich.
He can't go on supporting everybody.'

' He hasn't said anything, has he ? ' he asked anxiously.

' No—but——' I paused to enable him to say the
obvious.

' He wouldn't,' said Uncle Kostia. ' He is wonderful.
I admire him.'

I returned to my coupé. It was evening now and the
lights were lit. Dismal forests stretched over hundreds of
versts. I lay back and the ideas let loose by Uncle Kostia
set to work in my mind. And I thought : Where are we
heading ? Why ? What is it all for ? And then I thought
of the war with its hysterical activity ; I pictured soldiers
boarding trains, to return to the front ; the loading of ships
with war material ; the rush in the Ministry of Munitions.
I thought of the Germans seething with energy in just the
same way ; and I contrasted in my mind this hustling

activity, this strained efficiency with the pitiable weakness in the intellectual conception of the conflict, and I understood that the man had been essentially right, that our journeys were in excess of our achievements. Our life was an inept play with some disproportionately good acting in it. Then, as I dreamed away, I heard Fanny Ivanovna talking to somebody in the adjoining coupé. I pulled my door open and I could now hear her voice distinctly. I listened. I was vastly tickled. I wondered to whom it was that she was telling her autobiography. Then I heard occasional expressions of assent in Sir Hugo's trim and careful Russian. I leaned forward, the incarnation of attention.

\*     \*     \*     \*     \*

' He would come to me in the evening and say, " Fanny, I don't know what I would do without you. . ."

\*     \*     \*     \*     \*

' He came to me one evening in April and said, " Fanny, I must speak to you very seriously. . ."

\*     \*     \*     \*     \*

' " It is love, this time, real love. I thought that I had loved, I *had* loved, *you*, Fanny, but this is the love that comes once only, to which you yield gloriously, magnificently, or you are crushed and broken and thrust aside. . ." '

\*     \*     \*     \*     \*

I felt my heart beat violently within me. I waited for Sir Hugo's detailed cross-examination ; but indeed there was little of it. Only once, when Fanny Ivanovna referred to Nikolai Vasilievich's wife did Sir Hugo stop her with an apology, to inquire ' *Which* wife ? '

The train rushed through the autumn night ; the windows now were black and revealed nothing. Interlacing with the din, squeal and rattle of the wheels, now and then my ear would catch familiar fragments of the monologue.

\* \* \* \* \*

' " Nikolai ! " I cried. " *Du bist verrückt . . . wahnsinnig ! . . .* "

\* \* \* \* \*

' I cried and he cried with me . . .

\* \* \* \* \*

' " Think of the children, Nikolai ! They are your children . . . "

\* \* \* \* \*

' I said to him : " I shall wait till you pay me off. I shall not leave otherwise." '

\* \* \* \* \*

I felt indeed I was on the summits of existence. Why should *I* be treated to such stupendous depths of irony ? There beyond the clouds the gods were laughing, laughing voluptuously. I could not sit still. With all my heart I craved to have a peep, if only at Sir Hugo's face. I thought I'd give my life to know what was his verdict on the situation. Noiselessly I stole into the corridor, and bending forward with infinite precaution, I peeped at the interior of the coupé. They sat next each other. Under the shaded light projected the ruddy weather-beaten face of Sir Hugo. Sir Hugo looked—how shall I describe it ?—he looked as if he thought it was a case of damned bad staff work.

The train rushed on, noisily swaying through the silence of the night. I went back to my coupé, and passing Uncle Kostia's kennel I overheard the finale of what must have been a frantic theological discussion between Uncle Kostia and the General. The General, drunk, his fundamental principles of faith all uprooted and scattered in disorder about

the coupé, furious, with hair dishevelled, cried out to Uncle
Kostia :

'Well, *is* there a God, or *is* there no God ? '

'How do *I* know ? ' snapped Uncle Kostia angrily. 'Go
away ! '

## V

When the train arrived at Omsk, the new régime of
Kolchak had been established. The Admiral was distinctly
pleased with the change ; for he no longer believed in
granting the Russian people a Constituent Assembly because he had grounds for thinking that the Russian people,
if given this opportunity, would take advantage of it and
elect a government other than that of Kolchak. And the
Admiral was rather fond of little Kolchak, whose interpretation of democracy was that of denying the people the
choice of government until such time as by some vague,
mysterious, but anyhow protracted, system of education he
hoped their choice would fall upon his own administration.
We lived in our train, a verst or thereabouts from the
station—a thoroughly unwholesome place ; and the
Admiral diverted most of his time by throwing empty
tobacco tins at the pigs that dwelt in the ditches around the
train. ' You have no conception what a pig a pig really is,'
he said, ' till you see an Omsk pig.'

' Splendid ! ' said Sir Hugo. ' Splendid ! '

' There she goes again ! ' yelled the Admiral, and hit an
old big sow with a Navy Cut tobacco tin.

' Splendid effort ! ' said Sir Hugo. ' Splendid effort ! '

' I give dem h-h-hell ! ' roared General Bologoevski.
' Damrotten pigs ! ' But, as usual, his threat remained an
empty one.

But while most of us were very much at sea as to why
exactly we had arrived at Omsk, Nikolai Vasilievich seemed
immune from doubt. Nikolai Vasilievich, suspicious of the
punitive expedition, had arrived at the seat of the anti-

Bolshevik Administration to seek redress and compensation
in regard to his gold-mines. I think it was chiefly for my
British uniform that Nikolai Vasilievich asked me to
accompany him on his visit to the General at the General
Staff, before whom he was going to lay his case. I noticed
that Nikolai Vasilievich had always had a curious habit of
establishing some connexion between his personal grievance
and some powerful outside influence, as, for example, the
general question of Allied intervention; and he insisted
that he and we and intervention were really all one affair,
and that hence a favourable solution of his financial difficulties was all part and parcel of that scheme which aimed
at the defeat of Bolshevism.

We entered a large dirty waiting-room where crowds of
petitioners awaited their turn with a patience that bordered
on spiritual resignation : after the Russian manner they all
desired to see the head man personally, whose life was consequently spent in interviews. A nasty dirty little woman
with a nasty dirty little child, pointing at me with a dirty
finger, was saying to her howling offspring, in an attempt
to pacify her next-of-kin, ' Is that your daddy, is he ? Is that
your daddy ? '

The General was an elusive person, a wily man, a master
in the art of compromise. He was the idol of the Allies. He
was one of those few who could so wangle things, so balance
favours, as to please at once all the multitudinous Allies
and even curry favour with a large majority of Russians. His
habitual procedure was this. If an Ally asked him, for
example, for the allotment of a certain building, he always
promised without reserve. Then the Russian organization
in possession of that building would at once cry out in
protest; and he immediately assured them that they would
be allowed to keep the building : the whole matter, he explained, was a mere misunderstanding. Then the Russian
organization stayed, and when the Ally came to take the
building over they referred the Ally to the General. And
when the Ally came to him and asked for explanation, the

General, with a charming smile, would say, ' Well, you see that building is not really suitable for your use. I will find you a better one.' Then the Ally waited. He must have time, the General said ; and actually he played on time, on ' evolution.' And in the meantime there was a *coup d'état* ; or the Russian organization went bankrupt ; or the particular Allied representative who had been worrying him was replaced by another, with whom the General would begin again at the beginning ; or the Allied troops were about to be withdrawn ; or the city was recaptured by the Soviets ; or there was a fire and the correspondence was burned in the flames. He was a man who had no use whatever for ' free will ' and played entirely on ' predestination.'

The General listened to Nikolai Vasilievich's emotional narrative in a friendly manner, and smiling pleasantly he rose and shook hands, as if to show that the interview was at an end, saying, ' You may rest assured that it will be perfectly all right. Call again one of these days.'

Nikolai Vasilievich went out, beaming. ' Well,' he said, ' it seems settled.' I tendered my heartiest congratulations.

Then ' one of these days ' we called upon the General a second time. Nikolai Vasilievich laid great stress on the dastardly action of the Czechs—that nation just then being out of court with the government at Omsk—but the General merely said, ' Wait till the Supreme Ruler returns from Perm. I can do nothing without the Supreme Ruler.'

Nikolai Vasilievich then waited for the return of the Supreme Ruler ; and presently we called again. The General's manner, as he received us, was considerably less sunny than it had been on the two previous occasions. ' You have been here before,' he greeted Nikolai Vasilievich. ' You must have patience and wait.'

' *Wait ?* ' asked Nikolai Vasilievich in a tone of secret terror, the terror of a man who had been doing naught else all his life—and knew its meaning.

' Yes, I advise you to wait. Have patience.'

'How long?' asked Nikolai Vasilievich.

'How do I know?' the General replied. 'Wait—and you will see.'

Now, was it that Nikolai Vasilievich had waited long enough and seen nothing? Was it that in the circumstances he thought it sounded too much like a mockery? Or was it the explosion of that brewing restlessness that he had gathered in the years of intermittent waiting : the last puff of ineffectual remonstrance before his final sinking into hopeless resignation? But suddenly Nikolai Vasilievich went wild. I had never seen him in that state before. He abused the General in immoderate terms. He accused him first of turning honest people into Bolsheviks ; then of being in the pay of Moscow. He threatened to lead a rebellion against the Kolchak State. Nikolai Vasilievich ceased to be a man and became an incarnation : Man having lost his patience : Humanity gone wild in the waiting. He thundered forth at the adversary, and his ruined hopes were the woes of Humankind. Then, coming to the end of his intellectual resources, but far from having yet exhausted his spiritual wrath, he made reference to the Day of Judgment. The door into the chancery flew open, and the Chief of Staff, the Aide-de-camp, and heads of various departments, dashed upon the scene, wondering what on earth had happened ; and shouting loudly Nikolai Vasilievich hurled abuse upon the Chief-of-Staff, the Aide-de-camp, and the heads of various departments. And then in the waiting-room he went for a stray Admiral, a petitioner like himself, and hurled abuse at him as well.

'Very well,' the General said at length. 'Very well. If you won't be reasonable, I shall have to resort to the recognized procedure. Guard!' And he ordered them to take Nikolai Vasilievich away. Nikolai Vasilievich still raged and fluttered, and the guards came up to him with signs of deference and indecision. 'Come on, sir,' they persuaded him, 'he really means it.' And taking him each under one arm, they dragged him out into the open.

We walked back to the train.

'What those people will not realize,' I took it up to humour him, 'is that you can't live on nothing. Waiting doesn't feed you, and waiting doesn't clothe you ; and when you have a family——'

'Of course, one can borrow,' said Nikolai Vasilievich.

'Yes, of course,' I agreed.

Fanny Ivanovna greeted him with 'Well, Nikolai, is it all arranged ? '

A fiendish look came on his face, as though he said, 'The hell it is ! ' and all the more fiendish because he did not say it.

She sighed conspicuously. And her sigh gave him a nervous shudder. A look of hate came into his steel-grey eyes. 'She even sighs offensively,' he said to me, 'as though she meant to charge me with the necessity of doing so.'

'Nikolai ! ' she cried, 'don't let yourself go before strangers. What will Andrei Andreiech think of you ! You know I am not to blame because the mines won't pay. And you ought to remember that I advised you to sell them long ago, and if you had listened to me then we shouldn't have been in this plight. Well, well, it's no use quarrelling now. We've got to wait, that's all.'

The ironic fascination of the situation at this point proved irresistible. 'There's an English proverb,' I supplied : ' " All things come to him who waits." '

'Hm ! ' said Nikolai Vasilievich.

'And there's another one : " Rome wasn't built in a day." '

'Excellent proverbs ! ' he said dryly.

Kniaz popped his head out from behind the paper, like a mouse, and added, 'There's our own Russian proverb, too : " The slower you drive the farther you get." '

'You, Kniaz, had better read your paper,' retorted Nikolai Vasilievich acidly. 'What does it say in there ? '

I stood at the window of the stationary train and watched the sinking landscape dissolve in the gathering gloom about us. Why did the winter air seem so acutely strange, as if charged with something, a kind of tenderness, a warm, transfiguring love...? Nikolai Vasilievich came to my side and watched, his hands in his trouser pockets.

'Pigs in the ditches,' he brooded, 'pigs in offices, everywhere.—A town of pigs. That General—oh! what a pig...'

## VI

The 'affiliation' of Eisenstein into our 'society' was a tribute to his own unflagging perseverance. It so happened that while in Vladivostok the Admiral had been in urgent need of a dentist, and quite by accident he tumbled against Eisenstein, who had set up a practice there. The Admiral, though he loathed all Jews, was yet favourably impressed by Eisenstein because on his first visit to him he heard Eisenstein engage in a vigorous cursing of his Chinese servant. He liked to see a man who knew how to put 'these people' in their places, a man who knew how to assert his own authority, a man who did not talk about 'equality' and such-like tosh (discordant with his sentiment), 'utopia,' 'socialism,' and that sort of thing, you know, that has made the world, etc., etc. There was altogether too much Bolshevism abroad, and the vigorous action of the dentist with his Chink appealed to him unspeakably.

'This clamouring for allowing men from below to come up to the top and not imposing individuals of the old governing class from above,' he said. 'All damned well to talk like that, but in the meantime is anarchy to be allowed to continue unchecked? Apparently so.'

'Orright! Orright!' said Eisenstein.

This seemed the only word he knew in English. But it did not baffle him in the least; indeed he preferred to converse in English by means of its continual solitary use to any reasonable conversation in Russian; and when the Admiral spoke Russian to him he still replied, 'Orright! Orright!'

The Admiral had found him an amazing dentist. The Admiral's teeth and dentistry seemed the subject he was least interested in of all. He talked politics and finance. At intervals strange men and women of a strong Hebrew strain would run into the room, and Eisenstein, leaving the Admiral with his mouth wide open and cotton-wool stuck under his tongue, would exchange queries in a quick and agitated manner with these dark intruders. The Admiral would hear such phrases as ' What is the yen to-day ? How much is the dollar ? ' And if the Admiral chanced to touch the question of finance, Eisenstein would pounce upon him with inquiries : ' Do you want dollars ? How many dollars ? Or can I sell you francs ? ' Or suddenly he would ask the Admiral to recommend his being made a British subject. Where was the difficulty ? He could always change his name Eisenstein to Ironstone, which, he believed, sounded jolly well in English.

In a crisis he would suddenly drop his instruments on the floor and rely upon his naked hands, which by the way, he never washed between his clients. He was always one of two things : either extremely optimistic, when he said that the most violent pain was nothing ; or very pessimistic, when he said that nothing could be done to alleviate the pain. Sometimes he was extremely indolent and said that nothing was required to be done and all was well ; and sometimes violently enthusiastic for huge undertakings, for the most drastic and sweeping reforms, for extracting all the remaining teeth in the Admiral's mouth and substituting gold all over, and all sorts of crowns and bridges of his own invention that ran into four-figure dollars and were evidently going to hang loose in the Admiral's mouth. All the while he would talk and inflict his own political views on his clients, which were that the English were both fools and clever knaves : the apparent contradiction did not disturb him in the least ; and if the Admiral showed any inclination to contradict some amazing insinuation, he would just press the needle a little and manipulate it on the nearest nerve in

the tooth and so silence all opposition. He would talk of the
exchange at Vladivostok and of how easy it was to make
money, and when asked how to do it he would say you had
only to turn one currency into another, whether yen, dollars,
sterling or roubles, and a vast fortune was assured you,
evidently quite irrespective of the order of turnover, or the
particular currency, or the amount employed, or the rate at
which the transactions were being effected. He would talk
all the while, never stopping the whole time the client was
there ; and then at the finish stick a piece of saturated cotton-
wool into any hole in any tooth, take no heed of your
protests, and tell you to come again any time, any day—
when he would keep you waiting for whole hours at a
stretch. He would see you out, shouting in the passage in
reply to any question you might have put : ' Orright !
Orright ! ' as he closed the door upon you ; and then turn
to the next patient.

He attended to the Admiral's teeth twice in Vladivostok,
and then hearing through a third person that the Admiral
was not quite satisfied with the finality of his work, he left
the coast and joined the Admiral on his own initiative at
Omsk (in order to evade military service at the Base), and
now stated that he was a member of the Admiral's party.
He was followed by Baron Wunderhausen, now a second
lieutenant in Kolchak's Army, who arrived in Omsk and
asked the Admiral to take him on as his interpreter. This
was conceded. The young Baron, who said that he was
anxious to help, displayed a curious lack of judgment, or if
his aim was flattery, a curious ignorance of the art. He held
that Russia was a ' feminine ' nation, which should be con-
trolled and directed by a ' masculine ' nation like England ;
and that Great Britain should raise, equip, and officer an
army of Buriats, Khirghiz, Kalmucks, and other native races
in order to conquer Russia. As for himself, the Baron
wanted to wash his hands of the whole business, to get into
the British Army, to renounce his Russian nationality, and
get a post somewhere in Persia or Mesopotamia. It seemed

more and more as one lived longer that to get White Russia on her legs was like trying to get a feather-bed to stand on end.

Occasionally we would visit the front, and the Admiral would interfere in everything. He would look and shake his head : the pace and method of extermination would appear to him thoroughly inadequate. We stood behind a gunner who kept on firing at a tree, as such ; apparently for no other reason.

' What are you firing at ? ' the Admiral asked.

The man pointed at the tree.

' Are there any Reds behind ? '

The man shrugged his shoulders. The question to him seemed immaterial.

' Have you got a telephone there ? '

The man shook his head.

' But what are you aiming at ? '

He pointed at the tree.

It transpired that four regiments composing the division had gone over to the enemy that very morning. Of the division there remained just fourteen men, the Commander and his divisional headquarters, comprising about three hundred officers. We saw the Commander in his office and asked him what he thought he would do. He said that he would wait ; he thought the men might return.

' Who are you counting on,' said the Admiral sarcastically, ' God ? '

' Yes, Your Excellency,' sighed the Commander, ' we have no one else to count upon.'

And the Admiral felt shamed.

But the men, it seems, did not return. They ran as fast as their legs would carry them over to the Bolshevik lines, and the Bolsheviks, thinking that they were being attacked by overwhelming numbers, fled in disorder.

The Admiral was gloomy. The wind cut us in the face in our rapid drive. Slowly and gradually afternoon evolved into evening.

'That *Peking and Tientsin News*,' I broke the silence,
' seems to be somewhat pro-Bolshevik.'

' It's always pro-Something,' the Admiral grunted.

He looked out of the window of the car on the vast
snow-covered plains stretching all around us and brooded
darkly.

' Some people,' said he, ' think snow beautiful. I think
it idiotic.'

Although technically the presence of Nikolai Vasilievich's
family on our train was but a temporary measure, yet it was
recognized by all, through that deeper human instinct that
defies illusion, that there was an element of permanence
about it that would give points to the oak tree. Of course,
the Admiral could always have cleared his train of the family
by subjecting them to a prolonged machine-gun fire ; but,
as with soldiers, diplomats and politicians, the personal
morality of sailors is much above their national morality.
Need I say that they remained ? The motive of their journey
was that Nikolai Vasilievich was perpetually compelled to
see some General in some town along the line about his gold-
mines, for his gathering suspicions concerning the integrity
of the punitive expedition had now been amply justified.
And then, as time went on, the motive, as motives do, dis-
solved into a habit. But the relations between the Zina-
Uncle Kostia wing and that of Fanny Ivanovna and the three
sisters, and similarly, the relations between Fanny Ivanovna
and Magda Nikolaevna, were far from satisfactory. At
wayside stations and impromptu halts in fields and glades
and valleys, when we all left the train and hastened to take
exercise, there had been awkward situations ; and when the
three sisters had occasion to pass Zina or any of her little
sisters they never failed to put out their tongues at them—
presumably as a sign of disapproval of Nikolai Vasilievich's
approval of them.

We parted with them as we got back to Vladivostok ;
but they continued coming to our parties ; and the rumour

spread that Fanny Ivanovna was, as they say, *bien vue* at the Admiral's ' Court.' Only once, the very haughty wife of an insignificant officer, newly landed at the port, sounded the alarm : ' A *Problem* has arisen in *Society* ! *Can* we receive a German, or *can* we not ? ' But the problem, like so many problems, died its death without solution.

## VII

It was the day after General Gaida's unsuccessful rising. ' They've gone out for a walk with those three American naval officers,' Fanny Ivanovna told me when I called. ' Just the two of us, as usual,' she added somewhat bitterly. Kniaz, seated in the corner, audibly confirmed her statement, as it were, by sucking sweets. There was an acute scent of eau-de-Cologne in the room.

' How charming ! ' I exclaimed, bending forward to examine a tiny little jumper that she was knitting.

' Oh, that's for my godchild.'

' Who ? '

' Oh, the little girl I christened. Madame Olenin's little daughter. She's just three weeks old to-day. A dear little thing.'

' Another niece for Uncle Kostia, what ! They do turn them out in that family. Zina has more cousins than any girl alive ! '

' Well,' said Fanny Ivanovna, ' the little thing can't help being her cousin. And Madame Olenin is really very nice. What does it matter after all if she's her aunt ? I respect her all the same, and she did so want me to be the godmother, and the little girl is called Fanny after me.'

The canary hopping to and fro punctuated the swift movement of her accustomed fingers.

' My dear Andrei Andreiech,' she burst out in answer to my question as to when Nikolai Vasilievich would be back, ' there was a time when I knew all about his movements.

But that time is over. I feel more and more as we live longer that my hold on him is weakening. And I feel with every day it's getting weaker and weaker, and he is slipping away from me, and I am powerless to stop him. And soon I shall cease to bother altogether. He can stay there all night if he pleases.'

' I've seen Zina lately. She looks quite grown up.'

' Oh, what a headache I have ! ' She dipped her folded handkerchief into a bowl of eau-de-Cologne and pressed it to her forehead. ' If I hadn't Nina to console me.—Oh, you have no idea what a tender, loving heart our Nina has.'

' Nina *tender* ? '

' You don't know her. Do you remember that day you arrived here, and I was so anxious to know where she had been ? Well, she wouldn't tell me then because . . . she thought it might upset her plan. Afterwards she told me. She had been to see her mother.'

' Is that all ? '

' Well, it seems her mother wants to make it up with me —wants, in fact, that we should start a business together. Hats.'

' And won't you ? '

She thought for a time. ' I don't think I could,' she said at last, ' after what she's *said* about me.'

There was a pause of silence, which the canary, though, did nothing to observe. ' But if I do, it will be solely for Nina's sake. Poor child, she so wants to make our peace.'

' But doesn't Sonia, as the eldest sister, ever take the lead ? '

' Sonia ? ' She laughed. ' Why, look at Sonia. We have a nickname for her—" Miss Moon." It suits her admirably. And Sonia is deceitful. Yesterday she lied to me. She said that they had been to see their mother, but as a matter of fact Nina told me afterwards that they had gone to a dance on the American cruiser with Mr. Ward and White and Holdcroft.'

' What, again ! '

' Yes, I am very much against it,' she confided. ' I was furious. I said to Nina : " Andrei Andreiech and your father had nearly lost their lives looking for you everywhere during the firing." But all she said was, " There was no need to." '

' They had been on the American Flagship . . . on the American Flagship . . .' My mind could not digest the news. Yesterday when the firing had begun, Nikolai Vasilievich rushed in, panic-stricken, and said that the three sisters had been lost in the upheaval. I had been sitting in the little office with Sir Hugo, who was writing to a Czech Colonel of his acquaintance to apologize for mis-spelling the Colonel's name in a recent letter. This done, Sir Hugo looked through some old minutes of past meetings to see if there was any matter which had not been quite thoroughly thrashed out. He thought he was about to find such a matter, when a rifle report echoed sharply through the air, and was immediately followed by a multitude of others. We rose and looked out of the window. The projected *coup* had broken out.

There was a continuous rattle of machine-gun fire. The station building and the square before it were being attacked by Gaida's men and defended by British-trained cadets from Russian Island School. A fearless cadet in British khaki lay on the bridge that traversed the rails, fully exposed to view, and rattled off his machine-gun ; then he lay still. Several bodies were already lying on the square, some dead, others wriggling with pain.

Most of the remaining family had been removed to an empty barracks near the station before fighting had become desperate. But it was not till we had launched into the streets that we asked ourselves how we proposed to set about our task. On we walked, looking in at stray houses, inquiring at private flats ; but I think at heart we realized that our action was more by way of satisfying our con-sciences, for we had not a ghost of an idea where to look for them. Returning, we perceived the two mothers lamenting bitterly the death of the same children (which they had been quick to take for granted)—but still not on speaking terms with each other. A window had been knocked out by a stray shell.

Firing subsided and then resumed and grew in intensity, as darkness descended upon the town. A drizzling November snow now fell upon the wrangling troops. The station changed hands more than once. Some wounded men had been picked up and dragged into a hospital rigged up in the barracks and were heard moaning and groaning the long night through, while the city shook under fire of field-guns.

The morning unveiled a gruesome picture. The snow that had fallen in the night, and was still falling, now covered the ground and its dead bodies some inches deep. The square, the streets, the yards, the rails, and sundry ditches betrayed them lying in horrid postures, dead or dying. Those that were not dead, when discovered were finished with the bayonet by the ' loyal ' troops, amid unspeakable yells. Then they lay still and stiff in horrible attitudes. Men and women would stoop over them, gaze and wonder. Perhaps there is nothing that brings home so clearly the conviction of the temporary nature of human things as the sight of a dead body. What a moment since had been a human being with a life and purpose of his own was now an object, like a stone or a stick.

' I shall not forget that night,' said Fanny Ivanovna, ' nor what I saw this morning. The faces of the prisoners, some almost green from fright, as they stood with their hands up in the cold grey light of the morning, and the babyish face of that Cossack subaltern—a veritable mother's darling—as he detailed them into two parties. And then that other boy of about the subaltern's own age, awfully good-looking, who had been hiding in the chimney all night and was forgotten and only remembered as the prisoners had been marched off to the station to be killed. Then came that terrible rattle of machine-guns from within. He was hurried

up to the boyish subaltern who motioned in an off-hand
manner in the direction of the station ; and then a soldier
ran across with him—the soldier in front, the boy following
—hastening to be in time for the firing-party. But the firing
had just that moment come to an end. The boy fumbled in
his pocket and gave some folded paper to the soldier ; then
vanished into the station. And some moments afterwards
there came those three solitary shots.'

' When I entered the station,' I said, ' I saw piles of dead
bodies lying on the steps on which rich red blood trickled
down all the way ; and on top of all that handsome boy,
with the back of his scalp blown off. They were shot at by
machine-guns as they were being driven down the stone
staircase in the station, and their boots had been removed
and appropriated by their executioners. One man three
hours afterwards was still breathing heavily. He lay on the
steps, bleeding, and covered by other bleeding bodies.
Another man in the pile was but slightly hit. He lay alone
in the pile of dead, with a curious mob and sight-seeing
soldiery walking about him, shamming death. After three
hours he rose and walked away, but was caught and shot.'

' Horrible ! ' she said. ' It's shameful ! The Whites kill
the Reds, the Reds kill the Whites—and nobody is any the
farther. If people would only realize that killing is the first
thing they shouldn't do.'

' The proposition would appear self-evident. But it seems
as if the one idea of the Kolchakites is bloodshed to suppress
bloodshed ; and that this also happens to be the idea of the
Bolsheviks ; and that the Kolchakites are shocked at it.'

' Why can't human beings settle things by conference ? '

' They must be human beings for that, Fanny Ivanovna.'

' Sir Hugo surely——'

' Sir Hugo's chief preoccupation at a conference is to
commit another allied gentleman into saying " Yes " on any
given point, and then by a series of masterful, elaborate and
elusive thrusts of speech to commit him into saying " No " ;
and then to point out the contradiction. It is what Sir Hugo

calls " displaying the good old fighting spirit." His attention is essentially devoted to the careful recording of documents that find their way into our office accidentally, documents which in themselves he regards as inessential and
unimportant. And the Admiral hates Sir Hugo's love of
detail and exactitude which seems bent on proving to him
very clearly and precisely the uncertainty and vagueness of
his own position.'

She sighed.

' It is a consolation,' said she, ' to think that there are
other useless people in the world besides ourselves.'

The snow still fell in heaps as I walked home, and it grew
markedly colder, and one felt the onset of winter ; while
prisoners, it was said, were being killed in prison—noiselessly—out of consideration for the Allies in the city.


# VIII

Who can convey at all adequately that sense of utter
hopelessness that clings to a Siberian winter night ? Wherever else is there to be found that brooding, thrilling sense
of frozen space, of snow and ice lost in inky darkness, that
gruesome sense of never-ending night, and black despair
and loneliness untold, immeasurable ? Add to this the
knowledge of a civil war fumbling in the snow, of people
ill-fed, ill-clothed and apathetic, lying on the frozen ground,
cold and wretched and diseased. A snowstorm is blowing
furiously ; the wooden house groans and yells in the night ;
the tin roof squeals in agony, fearful lest it be cast to the
winds ; and the storm now howls like a beast, now sobs like
a child, now dies away, gathering for another outburst.

The house was lit and warm and comfortable. It was the
Admiral's house. But the Admiral was away, and in his
absence I had conceived it possible to give a dinner-party.
The arrangement of the guests at table had been a delicate
but delicious business. I had placed Fanny Ivanovna at the

side of Magda Nikolaevna. I had seated Nikolai Vasilievich
side by side with Eisenstein. I had sprinkled some of Zina's
sisters amongst the three sisters. And there was Sir Hugo,
who talked in French about the Russian situation to Zina's
mother (who feared God, and knew no French); and it
was evident, moreover, as he talked that his daily paper was
not the *Daily Herald* but rather the *Morning Post*.

The table was littered with bottles of the very best wine,
procured from the Admiral's private cellar, and the expression of my guests became, as they do become under the
influence of wine, more impulsive and less amenable to the
control of the will. Their will seemed, as the feast proceeded, to become less and less amenable to the authority of
the conscience. Kniaz had been drinking cocktails wholesale. He had never tasted one before, and found that his life
had been wasted. ' They are exquisite,' he said.

' They are,' Sir Hugo said. ' They induce one to forget
their price. Oh, no, no ! I didn't mean it in that way, Prince.
Do have another cocktail.'

I sat still among my guests, strangely flushed, and the vast
sea of Russian life seemed to be closing over me. I saw
Fanny Ivanovna talking to Magda Nikolaevna, somewhat
timidly perhaps and with undue reserve, but still *talking* !
Eisenstein was gleaming with silent satisfaction as he surveyed ' the family.' He felt, I think, that he was one of it at
last, and now he was all right. Nikolai Vasilievich on more
than one occasion addressed Eisenstein as ' Moesei
Moeseiech ' in an amiable if not familiar *sotto voce*. Zina's
mother spoke very eagerly to Sir Hugo about the persecu-
tion of the Russian priesthood by the Bolsheviks, but much
of her eloquence was lost upon him. Sir Hugo's knowledge
of her language, in spite of his long residence in Russia, was
inexplicably remote. When he was asked if he could talk
Russian well, he would say ' Moderately.' But, as a matter
of fact, his ability to express himself in Russian was, I think,
confined to hailing a cab in that language by crying out the
word ' Izvozchik,' and then, seated therein, muttering the

word ' Poshol ! ' which he usually mispronounced as ' Push
off '—both words happily meaning literally the same thing
and so adequately similar in sound as to serve his purpose.

General Bologoevski, on my left, was holding forth on
the situation.

' Looks pretty hopeless,' I remarked.

' Not a bit of it,' rejoined the General.

' But they are retreating everywhere.'

' On purpose,' said the General.

' But whatever for ? '

' Well, there was a conference of generals—I presume—
who have decided it. I think it a good thing myself.'

' Why ? '

' Well—we'll entrap them.'

' I am most pessimistic.'

' I am perfectly optimistic—quite certain of victory.'

' Why, General ? '

' Denikin.'

' He is advancing very slowly.'

' Ah, but he is about to enter Great Russian territory.'

' Well, what's there in that ? '

' Why,' he explained, ' the Great Russians are the only
real decent Russians. I am a Great Russian myself.'

I nodded with significance, as if to indicate that this made
all the difference to the situation.

Then, once again, Fanny Ivanovna sat silent. Perhaps
she thought of her position, insecure and unconventional,
disused, no longer wanted ; and of her instincts so discordant with her life, her instincts that had always been on
the side of respectability, the purity of home life, the sanctity
of marriage, and the very things, in fact, that had always been
denied her : so much so that in her unstable, questionable
position she had yet been stringently insistent on this aspect
of their life, and always in her heart was reminded that she
had no title to enforce that law, no claim, beyond a doleful
craving for the decencies of usage and convention. Perhaps
the presence of Nikolai Vasilievich's two other wives had

served to remind her of the painful irony of her life ; perhaps the wine affected her with melancholy as it had affected
me. Perhaps she pondered on her broken life, her sacrifices
that had gone unnoticed ; or pictured to herself her eventual
return to Germany, the cruel astonishment of those for
whom she too had sacrificed her life. And it may have
occurred to her, as a belated afterthought in life, that
possibly she had been ' sat upon ' too often and too much.

But no ; it was not quite that. There was something
fatalistic, and yet almost defiant, in her look. A blend of
optimistic resignation. What was it ? What was she dis-
covering ? Why that smile ? It was as though in desperation she had given him full rein and found, to her amazement, that he did not seem to pull as hard as when she held
him tight.

I perceived that my dinner-party promised well. I caught
Fanny Ivanovna's eye and raised my glass ; and instantly I
had her glass refilled. My head began to swim. I discovered
an agreeable warmth in my body, and the expression that
had come on my face seemed to be getting out of my control.
' Fanny Ivanovna,' I cried, ' never mind my expression :  I
know it is stupid. It has come on of its own accord, and I
cannot quite remove it, though I feel that a smile may
develop of itself at any moment.'

' Look,' Nina said to Sonia, ' how awfully funnily his
face changes from smile to seriousness. Look ! '

I smiled a drunken smile.

' Look : there again ! '

I should have explained here that I had a passion for that
white and pasty substance that Russians eat at Easter—
paskha, and when I was in Russia I made it my habit to eat
it in and out of season. I had a pyramid of considerable
dimensions locked up in the safe.—And now, at the
close of dinner, the secret was betrayed. A dash was made
for it. The guests armed themselves with knives, forks, and
spoons and dug into the substance and cleared it away in
less than twenty minutes. They then lay moaning and

suffering not a little from its effect on their abounding stomachs.

We were jolly, exuberant, self-centred and sentimental. I felt distinctly pleased with myself. I knew not why ; that is the secret of good wine. Some people laughed, others after the manner of the Slav were fain to weep ; and outside there raged the snowstorm of a Siberian winter night.

Fanny Ivanovna, Magda Nikolaevna, Čečedek, Eisenstein, Nikolai Vasilievich, reclined on sofas and arm-chairs, smoked and sipped liqueurs ; and Sonia, Nina, Vera, Zina and her sisters and Baron Wunderhausen made a noise in the adjoining rooms and did wild things with the furniture.

Uncle Kostia stood on the hearth-rug, dazed and very red in the face, and held forth at great length : his Russian soul a reservoir of overflowing feeling. ' I feel positively strange,' he said. ' I swear I never felt like this before. I nodded, do you know, to some point in an argument with which at the time I happened to agree, and to my great embarrassment I somehow kept on nodding quite in spite of myself, and keep on nodding—do you see me, Fanny Ivanovna ?—though the portion of the argument with which I had expressed agreement long died in oblivion. I know it is the wine. It is good wine, and—to make a long story short—I am drunk. But I don't care. This is an exceptional night. It is a memorable night. Fanny Ivanovna and Nikolai Vasilievich and Magda Nikolaevna, Moesei Moeseiech, Zina, Sonia, Nina, Vera, Kniaz : I swear I never felt so near to you as I do feel to-night. I feel beastly sentimental. I feel that I could howl aloud. I feel that presently I will go round and kiss each one of you in turn. Look into your own hearts. What is the use of pretending ? We are all one family and Nikolai Vasilievich, our dearly beloved, much-respected Nikolai Vasilievich, is our parent and guardian. He stood by us well in our hour of need. His task has been an uphill task ; but has he complained of us ? Not once. He has borne the burden of many families without a sigh of protest. Speaking for myself, we men of letters have to lean for our support on stalwart men like Nikolai Vasilievich, and it is indeed largely on their generous help that art and literature must depend. As you know, we men of letters are no business men, but if as a writer and a student of life and human nature I may presume to give advice : don't lose courage, Nikolai Vasilievich. Remember, we are all behind you ; we shall follow you, if need be, to the end of the earth. Courage, Nikolai Vasilievich ! Keep hard at it ! Keep hard at it ! '

We became agitated. We all spoke at once, perhaps for no other reason than that we had been deprived of speaking for so long. And then, suddenly, we subsided, for on the floor above us, occupied by a Russian family, someone was playing the piano. It was Chopin. We listened to the music and grew still, and our souls were all music as though he had touched their strings. And the house seemed charmed, and the gruff Siberian night looked in through the window and listened in silence... For his is the grace and sweet melancholy of romance, and his the laughter of silver trumpets, and tears as bright as the dew at dawn. His sorrows are no graver than the sorrow of the gold-red sunset, and his sobs are the sobs of the sea, the echo of the waves weeping on the rocks. And it has all been to him a dream in music, and when we hear it we dream with him...

' And Fanny Ivanovna,' said Nikolai Vasilievich, ' is now a widow ! '

A thought flashed across my brain. ' Fanny Ivanovna,' I cried, ' I had meant to ask you what was that funeral procession you all followed yesterday ? '

' My husband's,' she said, and I was struck unpleasantly by her tone of mirth and triumph.

' Eberheim ? '

' Yes,' smiled Nikolai Vasilievich ; ' she is a widow now. A *merry widow* ! ' And Fanny Ivanovna laughed in a loud and jarring manner. It seemed odd why I had not guessed so obvious a candidate when I had seen the funeral procession pass by my window, and had supposed that the corpse had been some victim of the Gaida outbreak. We all felt that it was the best thing for the man, and nothing more was said on the subject. Eisenstein, in an impossible condition, sang sentimental gipsy songs to his own accompaniment on the piano, and his voice was such that the cat hid itself in the house and could not be found for three days afterwards ; and Nikolai Vasilievich was assisting him in a rather timid staccato baritone. Sonia, Nina, Vera, Zina and her sisters, Baron Wunderhausen and I were dancing in the adjoining room. Fanny Ivanovna and Magda Nikolaevna, seated side by side on the sofa, were discussing, somewhat timidly it seemed, Magda Nikolaevna's proposal that they should start a millinery establishment together, procuring fashionable ' Parisian ' hats from Peking and Shanghai and selling them at great profit in Vladivostok ; and Zina's father was sleeping, mouth wide open, in his chair.

## IX

She was going along quickly, wrapped in the familiar fur ; and it was snowing merrily.

' Nina ! '

She turned round and stopped, smiling. And the bright white winter day seemed to be smiling with her. It was the day of the Social Revolutionary *coup d'état*. Early in the morning troops of revolutionary partisans had occupied the city peacefully, and taken possession of the public buildings, to wild cheering from the local crowds. The Russian national flag had been hauled down and a red one hoisted in its stead. Processions had appeared with revolutionary banners, and the town was decorated in red. ' Have you heard the news ? ' she said. ' Pàvel Pàvlovich, the Baron, has fled to Japan overnight, without telling us a word.'

' Of course, he was in danger of being arrested by the Reds,' I said. ' But I suppose he'll come back some day.'

She shook her head. ' I don't think so.'

' What does Sonia think ? '

' She's glad.'

' *Glad?* '

' Yes. She was going to leave him herself—to marry Holdcroft. But now——'

' Now what ? '

' But now *he's* left her.'

' Well, all the better, then. Saves trouble.'

' It's . . . humiliating.'

We went on together and, nearing home, we cut through masses of new snow. It was one o'clock. The sun shone yellow. She put her hand into my coat pocket. Tender flecks, falling from the sky, would linger on her brows and lashes. We fumbled and wrangled in the snow ; and, with that bird-like look of hers, she said, ' To-day . . . I like you.'

At the American Headquarters dance last night she had been strangely, inexplicably hostile ; and Fanny Ivanovna had made it worse by exhorting her to dance with me against her will. And, of course, there were Ward and White and Holdcroft. I remember sitting there that night with a sense of injury. What was the matter ? Had I usurped too many of her dances ? I felt as a man might feel who in a moment of particular goodwill towards mankind discovers that his watch has been pickpocketed. I said nothing, but strove to put it all into my look. She came up to me, rapturous, delicious. There was about her that night a disquieting, elusive charm. ' I told you that I love you. What else do you want ? ' She said it with just that torturing proportion of smile and earnestness that you could not tell how it was meant : and very likely that was just how it was meant. I remember I ransacked my soul for something stinging. ' You can't love,' I said. ' You're not a woman ; you're a fish.' It is unfair to analyse love-reasoning unless in a similar emotional temperature. The dance over, our coats on, we sat and waited for the car, Nina looking rather sulky. —And to-day what a change the sunshine has wrought !

We reached their house. ' Come in,' she said.

' No.'

She went in, took off her coat, and while I lingered, came back and stood on the steps.

' You'll catch cold like that.'

She shook her head.

' I wish,' said I, ' that women would propose to men. I should love to say, " Oh, why can't we remain just friends ? " '

She looked at me. ' You would say it to *me* ? '

' Jokingly, of course.'

' I shan't propose then.'

' And if I said it seriously, would you propose then ? '

' Yes,' she laughed.

' Aren't we supposed to be engaged, though ? '

' Are we ? '

' I think so.'

' We'll marry but divorce at once,' she said, ' and live separately, and meet only once a year.'

And then the door opened and Nikolai Vasilievich said somewhat angrily to me : ' Either come inside, or go. She'll catch cold standing here with nothing on.' And as he vanished he rather slammed the door.

' Go in, Nina, or he'll be angry.'

' Take no notice of him. None of us take any notice of him. That's why he is angry.'

' Then I'll go in,' I said. And we both went in, and heard Fanny Ivanovna saying : ' Believe me, Sonia, it's all for the best. If you like, send him a post-card with " Good riddance " on it. That's all you need say.' And as I listened, it transpired further—for misfortunes never come alone— that Baron Wunderhausen was not a baron, and not even Wunderhausen.

Sonia was downcast. ' What the devil does it matter, anyhow,' argued Nikolai Vasilievich, ' above all now that he is gone, whether he is a baron or no baron, Wunderhausen or no Wunderhausen ? ' But Sonia would not hear of it. That he should have left without telling her a word !

That he should have lied to her all these years ! Also she
had always scoffed at him for his title, thought it ridiculous,
almost a deliberate affectation. But now that the truth had
been revealed to her and she knew that he had never had a
title, she felt that she had been insulted rudely, married
under false pretences. Well, she would insist on a divorce ;
she would take good care that she was the first in the field
to insist on it. Holdcroft was extraordinarily attractive. He
seemed rather keen on Vera, though. But how beautifully
he danced.

And just that moment the gramophone, which Vera was
fiddling with, broke loose into an intoxicating one-step.
Nina, standing by it, echoed at the end of each refrain—
' My-y-y *cell*-ar ! ' as the music galloped into syncopation.

' Whose is the gramophone ? '

It was Olya Olenin's, the timid ' football ' little niece of
Uncle Kostia.

' There they are ! ' cried Sonia. Three U.S. naval uniforms
appeared in the window.

' If only we had more room here,' sighed Fanny Ivanovna.
But how scrupulously clean she kept the little that there was
of it.

' *I'*m for ever *blow*-ing bub-*bles*,' hissed the gramophone...

' *Fu*—fu fu fu *fu*—fu fu——' whistled Nikolai Vasilievich.
And, forgetful of her prodigal baronial spouse, Sonia
dodged the chairs and sofa in the embrace of Holdcroft,
while Kniaz sat in his corner seat, a little in the way, and read
his paper and sucked sweets.

' You want to go ? ' Fanny Ivanovna looked at Nikolai
Vasilievich with a solicitude that suggested a desire to
anticipate his wishes. ' All right. We'll have our tea now.
Sonia ! Nina ! Vera ! Tea.'

' There's no hurry,' he calmed her.

During tea he was hilarious. He had been out in the
streets and mixed with the crowds. What hilarious, happy
crowds ! The change had come about at last. Something
would happen *now*. He said he thought it would be a few

days only till the thing was finally settled. He meant to go and see some of the new ministers. A quite decent Government, it seemed ; and what good order, all things considering. The Social-Revolutionaries had a double platform ; they appealed to those who had no use for international militarism on revolutionary grounds, and to those who had no use for revolution on national grounds. And Nikolai Vasilievich thought that such broad-minded, reasonable people could not fail to see his point as regards the gold-mines. I sat listening to him and in my influx of sudden happiness eating more than I really wanted to ; for I felt she was *à moi* once more.

He went out at last, and Fanny Ivanovna shut the door behind him. She looked at me, smiled, and then heaved a little sigh. ' I let him do as he pleases,' she said. ' Perhaps it's better so. We'll see...'

As it darkened we took Olya home, and trailing our feet in the deep snow, carried the uncomfortably heavy gramophone, and marched in various formations, halted, marched again, and then, towards the climax, carried Nina in a burial procession. At the Olenins we danced again, I claiming Nina and the three American boys having to put up with what was ' second best.' Madame Olenin, a suckling in a jumper at her breast, stood in the doorway and watched. A ten-year-old military cadet had followed her into the room and also stood in the doorway, in a civilian overcoat, and gaped at us. 'Our Peter,' said she, ' is a loyal little monarchist and refuses to take off his shoulder-straps in spite of the Red *coup d'état*.' The maternal hand stroked the offspring's hair in a tender gesture. ' But I made him put on this civilian overcoat on top. It isn't safe, you know.'

I came up and cuddled little Fanny in a rather inefficient fashion and lavished unmitigated praise, as is the classic way when talking to a mother of her babe. And then little Fanny, as is the classic way with babies, for no apparent cause, began howling, howling without rhyme or reason. I was made to play the piano, and I was pleasantly aware that Nina advertised me and showed me off as though I was her own special merchandise. The snow in the yard was pink from the sun as we jumped about on the sofa. She took water in her mouth and blew it out into my face, whereon I got her into a corner and slapped her hard, while the others looked on in amusement. She was trying to bite my hands ; and then as we went out she *would* insist on fastening my overcoat.

The others trailed behind, and we could hear their laughter growing fainter as we walked ahead. The snow creaked agreeably beneath our feet. It was five o'clock and there were the first signs of twilight. We passed the sombre silhouette of their little wooden house. Oh, how sad were these things in the winter... Darkness was swiftly setting in. We crossed the wood. The tall pine-trees, covered with a thick coating of snow, stood mute and dreaming in the twilight ; only their peaks moved ever so gently to and fro, murmuring some vague complaint.

Then, suddenly, we came out into the open and saw the sea. Clad in an armour or ice, it was as smooth as a mirror. Here and there a monstrous snow-covered lump rose from the surface. The sky was grey and fretful and darkness fell upon us with every minute. The sun, as it set, slowly cast a feeble red flame on the sea chained in ice, and the crescent moon spread a yellow light over the surface, glimmering in varied colours on the ice, the snow, the glaciers. The wind strengthened and the frost pricked at my ears.

' Say something ! Say something ! '

' What shall I say ? '

' Why, you're worse than Kniaz ! ' I exclaimed.

She smiled.

' Say that the sea is a dazzling sight, that the moon is— well, anything you like, that the sun is red copper.'

She looked as though all this was nothing, but she alone was real. ' Why falsify the tone ? It's there : I can see it.'

' Is this not beautiful ? You're an amazing creature ! One doesn't know which side to get hold of you. I talk to you about—about—*this* ' (a florid gesture to the sea). ' You tell me it is false.'

' *This* ' (an imitative florid gesture) ' is all right. But please don't talk about it to me.'

She was silent.

' I liked you this morning,' she said then. ' But *now*——! '

' You see, the trouble is,' said I, ' that you can't talk of anything but fox-trots.'

' Last night at the American dance,' she said, ' I danced with Ward.'

' I know, I saw you,' I said in a tone of condemnation.

' He's very nice ; I like him ; but I can't talk of anything to him. He asked me, " Do you like fox-trots ? " I said, " Yes." And when later on we danced the waltz, he said, " Do you like waltzes ? " And I said, " Yes." And he said, " I like them too." '

' There you are ! ' I cried triumphantly. ' You've got to stick to me and sack all the rest ! '

' You are nice,' she said, ' and there are days when I like you—though *you* never know when they are. But . . . I can't talk to you.'

And she added, ' I am going home.'

The sun contracted and grew more red and feeble as the moon shone brighter and cast an even yellow light upon the space around us. Fretful fantastic shadows flitted across the ice. Objects about us grew black. Darkness was now hard upon us.

We returned by moonlight that glimmered on the snow.

## X

Six weeks elapsed, and the snow was melting in the valley. When the sun appeared behind the trees the birches, steeped in water, had that silvery appearance which is beautiful beyond measure. Spring was in the air.

It was a dinner, a formal, drunken, tedious affair that I must needs attend. I sat between General Bologoevski and a British flag-lieutenant, who had fallen in love with Nina at first sight and now drank in greedily everything I had to say about her. In this building, not so long ago, other men had met their death. At each *coup d'état* this house had been besieged. Fugitives had taken shelter in these rooms. Even on this sofa a body had been stabbed to death. And now we revelled noisily. The dark, dark night of early spring was a breathing, watching presence. The bare white-plastered walls seemed to prick their ears.

What had happened ? Nothing. The nights were drawing in. The three sisters had gone to a dance. And so had Ward, White and Holdcroft. When now I called on them, more often I would find the older folks alone. How melancholy, but strangely fascinating, were these evenings : this gathering of souls dissatisfied with life, yet always waiting patiently for betterment : enduring this unsatisfactory present because they believed that this present was not really *life* at all : that *life* was somewhere in the future : that *this* was but a temporary and transitory stage to be spent in patient waiting. And so they waited, year in, year out, looking out for *life* : while life, unnoticed, had noiselessly piled up the years that they had cast away promiscuously in waiting, and stood behind them—while they still waited.

What Nikolai Vasilievich actually waited for was best known to himself. His hopes had been built up on the assumption of a sudden recovery of his gold-mines, a possibility he connected somehow with political developments in the Far East. It would not be fair to examine critically the grounds he had for this ambitious expectation, from any rational standpoint. Nikolai Vasilievich had built up enchanted castles of a rare magnitude and beauty upon this somewhat flimsy and elusive foundation ; and he could not have now examined this foundation with an open mind without ruining his dreams. And Nikolai Vasilievich had further committed himself to the continued sustaining of

illusions by identifying in his mind certain definite promises
of a financial nature that he had made to Zina and her
people, his daughters, Fanny Ivanovna, his wife and Kniaz,
with his dreams, indeed in such a manner that his dreams
had become vital realities to them; and this important consideration had served the further purpose of giving his
dreams all the more the appearance of realities. He had
private doubts, of course; but he brushed them aside in a
manly manner: he could not afford to do otherwise. He
waited for political changes. He was not clear in his mind
as to what particular political changes would serve his
purpose. He did not know. He was wise enough to know
that in conditions so complex and multitudinous as those
in Siberia there was no telling which particular political
combination would affect his gold-mines favourably. Moreover, he did not want to know. He did not want to know
because he felt that if he knew, his happiness henceforth
must needs depend on the single chance of that particular
political combination, alone likely to affect his gold-mines
favourably, coming into power; rather did he like to think
that his happiness depended on *any kind* of change on the
political horizon—a more than likely possibility.

At last he saw hopeful signs. The Social Revolutionary
partisans had occupied the city, and from day to day he
waited for an indication of their attitude towards his gold-
mines. This indication came to hand at last when they
called for him and put him into prison for having taken
part in that lamentable punitive expedition of which, as a
matter of fact, he was the chief victim. His term of im-
prisonment, unpleasant as it was, had yet served the good
purpose of further cementing his multitudinous family. His
daughters, Zina, Čečedek, Kniaz, Fanny Ivanovna, his wife,
Eisenstein, Uncle Kostia, Zina's father, and the book-keeper
Stanitski, all met in their frequent calls in the cell of the
breadwinner.

On dragged the dinner. General Bologoevski at my side
was telling me that he was at heart a democrat, that he

sincerely wished to see a government that was more democratic than the old ' damrotten government ' under the Czar.
Yes, his heart, he said, was democratic, and even when he
was in Tokio he could not suffer himself, yes, he could not
suffer himself (he put his hands upon his heart), big and
strong as he was, to be pulled by a dwarf slave. So he placed
the coolie in his ricksha and pulled the man himself. And
yesterday he went with his own Chink cook to a Chinese
theatre and sat out the whole performance in an incredible
atmosphere. Now was that not democracy ? And if it wasn't,
well, he questioned what democracy really was. He did his
bit. What else did the people want ? They were never
satisfied.

And then that unknown quantity, that strange old man
Sir Hugo, fired off a jewel. Sitting opposite, I could hear a
Captain of the U.S. Navy talking of the decline of discipline ;
to which Sir Hugo answered in his heckling manner, ' Well,
Captain Larkin, I don't think I can agree with you, and I
should be inclined, if you'll allow me, to suggest to you that
your people are not as disciplined as our men, or, should I
say, they have not had the same experience of discipline.'

' Well, may be yes ; may be no,' said the other. ' It seems,
though, Sir Hugo, they have done about equally well in the
war, anyhow.'

Whereon Sir Hugo was convulsed with merriment.
' Splendid fellow, Captain Larkin ! Good. Very good.
Splendid ! Ha, ha, ha, ha ! You're a diplomat, Captain
Larkin, you know. Oh, yes, you are. Very clever, very
diplomatic indeed. Ha, ha, ha, ha ! I notice you use just the
right word. Ha, ha, ha, ha ! You say " it *seems*." You're
not *committing* yourself, now are you, eh ? '

Captain Larkin ate his fish in silence. What was the world
indeed coming to ?

On dragged the dinner. The black panes of the big bare
windows stared unflinchingly. Yes, the three sisters had
gone to a dance with the three American boys ; and I could
picture to myself that other private little dance when I had

quarrelled with her deliberately, to bring matters to a head, to know where I stood. But the quarrel had not ' come off,' and her attitude was as ever unintelligibly vague. Then I sat there and watched her outline—what a girl !—and her side-long, bird-like look...

In came two Italian tenors, fingering their guitars. We leaned back in our chairs, watched the cigar smoke descend on the wine, listened how the southern mellow voices defied the breaking vigour of the night of early spring.

' To-morrow,' said the Flag-Lieutenant, ' at 7.30 comes the ice-breaker, and off we barge into the open.'

' To-o-re-e-*ador*——! To-o-rrre-ado-o-o-o-*or*! Tam-tram-taram-tam——'

' Two vermouths ! '

' That's the stuff to give 'em ! '

Hand upon heart, the singers emptied the glasses.

' Stenka Razin ! Stenka Razin ! The Russian robber song,' enjoined the table.

' *Ah ! je ne connais pas, messieurs.*'

And we sang the Russian robber song as best we could, and the Italianos both joined in as soon as they had got the hang of it. Dinner over, we sat about anyhow, and another soloist, a Hungarian prisoner of war, half-wailed, half-sobbed a Russian song that ended with the desperate refrain of ' Never, never, *never*, never . . . never. . . . ' The Russian General's eyes blinked in the cigar smoke. ' What's that play, you remember—" Those are not tears : it's the juice of my soul. The juice of my soul. . . . " ' Then the old Hawaiian band—we had been well provided for that evening—played ' *Tell me,*' by request.

' They played this at that dance,' said the Flag-Lieutenant. ' To-morrow at 7.30 we're off. I wonder if we shall ever come back.'

' Those are not tears : it's the juice of my soul...'

As we passed into the ante-room, the company was getting rowdy. A French Colonel, cigar in mouth, was throwing gramophone records on the floor, as though they were quoits, adding, with a blissful side-long smile at me, ' *Les disques !* ' Somebody had released the gramophone, and a rowdy one-step was the result. Cocktails, wine, liqueurs, whisky . . . 7.30, the ice-breaker, the juice of my soul, never, never, *les disques*. . . . Like dregs, they had been stirred from the bottom, swam up and began to flow hither and thither with the rolling of the tide. Abrupt impressions crowd my brain. Nina. Spring. A trip by motor to the Garden City. We lose our way. A bearded student of the intellectual brand offers to see us through, gets in next to the chauffeur and directs him, but presently loses his way too. ' This hill,' says he, as if to justify himself, ' used to be on the right bank of the river.' ' Heaven knows what's happened to it,' say I. She laughs. Oh, how she laughs ! We arrive at last—and, oh ! horror ! We meet her father and Zina. We lunch at the new Casino restaurant. The old proprietor shakes his clients by the hand respectfully, but bullies the waiters. It is Sunday. The sunlit sea, too, has a festive, leisurely appearance. We walk into a public park with the notice ' Cattle and Other Ranks not admitted.' Supper at the Casino restaurant. When evening comes the bullied waiters, conscious of the approach of the Red Army, demand a share in the profits in addition to their wage. The old proprietor shouts louder than he would and looks to the public for moral support. ' None of your Bolshevism here, please ! ' he shouts, putting on in emphasis what he lacks in weight ; and they can all feel that he is frightened of them. We talk to two Russian soldiers. One of them has never heard of Admiral Kolchak. ' You fool,' says the other, ' he's that English General who gives you clothing.' We return in the early evening. The sky is flushed ; the *datchas* steeped in foliage. The seaway sunlit route. Pink light everywhere. The approach of summer, the feeling that we should act in unison with nature, and the crushing, curbing sense that we dare not—oh ! for so many reasons. The waiting, the suspension of plans owing, among other things, to the civil war. The prevailing Russian atmosphere—

chronic uncertainty. The wild flowers in the grass at the road-side. The American regimental dance that night. She looks at me, sits near me. I help her on with her coat ; then to step into the car. And the nocturnal moonlit journey homeward. . . . Youth ! Her splendid, wonderful youth. How trivial, how great. How much, how little. That's how we live. A flash here ; a scent there. It's gone, and it's the devil to recapture.

The big black window-panes still stare at you indecently ; that's why somebody throws a bottle through them. The gramophone shoots painful memories through my feverish brain. Now she is dancing with them. . . . They are playing rugger with a crumpled piece of paper on the floor. Oh ! the pictures. Somebody has set a match to the imitation palm-tree. Good job ! And somebody else has poured a bottle of whisky into the piano. Uproarious shouts. A fat, flabby Major stands on the table, shouting ' Charing Cross. All change here ! ' and then begins to sell the furniture by auction and imitate a Bolshevik speaker all in the same breath. I am dragged up on the table. Shouts of ' Speech ! Speech ! ' My mouth begins to move but the voice seems to be coming out of an empty barrel ; both I and they seem someone else. The table begins to sway like a ship—a pendulum—and I feel that I am being supported on my legs only by some outward spirit. *Les disques.* The juice of my soul. Ha, ha, ha, ha ! I laugh feebly but awfully funnily, as I am being carried out under the arms. My room. Never, *never.* . . . Oh ! . . . The bed is a merry-go-round, a spindle. I dash out on to the floor. The floor revolves the other way. Damn ! Somebody ties a wet handkerchief round my head, and says, ' You're a brick. . . . ' Nina. *Les disques.* . . . Youth. . . . Your splendid, wonderful youth. . .

## XI

That evening I called on them to say good-bye, for we were leaving on the morrow. The occasion coincided with the release of Nikolai Vasilievich from prison, following on the seizure of the fortress by the Japanese. Already through the windows there gazed the evening of early spring. The church bells on that Easter Sunday, the most festal day in the year, rang dolefully through the Christian city seized by a heathen yellow race, and spoke of better days.

There had been another night of firing. The headquarters of the Russian Zemstvo had been fiercely bombarded in the night. Then when at last the building was stormed by Japanese troops they found, to their amazement, that there was no one there. General Bologoevski, who had been attached of late to the Russian Staff, discovered on the morrow that he had lost yet another government overnight. Down came the red flag and up went the flag of the Rising Sun. Russian prisoners tied to their Korean colleagues were being led through the streets on a rope, like cattle. Then, these lives wasted, this damage done, ' their honour satisfied,' as said the Nippon officers, they turned to the scattered government and invited them to return to their shattered offices and resume their interrupted duties. And Nikolai Vasilievich, released from prison, was inclined to think that the little Nippons were, on the whole, good fellows.

Fanny Ivanovna and he, alone in the house, were about to have tea. The canary in the cage seemed livelier at the approach of spring. The cat was growing fatter. The samovar could not be made to work. Nikolai Vasilievich, dressed up in a morning-coat, put on white leather gloves and blackened them considerably as he grappled inefficiently with the large insurgent samovar that blew up columns of black smoke in the little hall ; while Fanny Ivanovna, as usual, shouted advice to him from the adjoining room that really only served to annoy him.

' Sit down, Andrei Andreiech,' she said, ' he won't be long. Well, Nikolai,' she shouted, ' can you manage it ? Andrei Andreiech is *waiting* for his tea.'

' Shut up ! ' came his angry voice amid angry, recalcitrant hissing.

' Nikolai ! Please ! What will Andrei Andreiech think of you ? '

There was no *kulich*, no *paskha*. But Fanny Ivanovna had done up the table as well as she could for the occasion ; and there was something pathetic about the poor results she had attained compared with the lustre of pre-war Easter-week in Petersburg. We sat at table, and no one spoke. Nikolai Vasilievich was sad. Was he sad because he had returned from prison to something that was only prison in a mitigated form ? Was it that the suspense had been too long, that he had succumbed in the waiting ? Was it that he had suddenly, secretly, for no particular reason, on the eve of great changes, lost faith in the recovery of his mines ? Or was it just reaction, the unexpectedness of his release ? How much the one, how much the other, who can tell ? The emotion of the soul is an elusive thing. There is a subtlety about the moods that bears no introspection. These nights in early spring in Vladivostok are so intolerably sad that oft-times one might weep for no other reason than that life was passing untouched, unrealized, a drudgery with but a gleam of beauty.

Only later in the evening it transpired from his conversation that he hesitated. He hesitated what to do. His mind was in a state of perplexity and doubt. His finances were coming to an end. Should they all follow Baron Wunder-hausen to Yokohama on the off-chance that he has secured some post there ? But he remembered that the Baron was not a baron, and not even Wunderhausen, and he felt that he would be safer not to count on him. They might follow the Admiral to England, as the Russian General was doing ; or remain with Eisenstein in Vladivostok, who was begin-ning to succeed as a dentist here—there was a dearth of them—and wait till the mines materialize ? Perhaps he had better wait. Things seemed to be moving now at last, and perhaps there was more hope now than there had been hitherto.

After supper the Admiral and Sir Hugo came to say good-bye. Also, gradually, the family collected. The room was now full of people. The talk, as ever, lapsed into politics. The Russians have a habit of suspecting the ' Allies ' of unheard-of calumnies, so much so in fact that even the surprising attitude of innocence adopted by the allied representatives, who sincerely know no better, seems a fairer statement of the true position. The incentive to bloodshed in this miserable Russian business, as in fact the incentive to all murder, is not so much a matter of wanton wickedness as wanton ignorance : a metaphysical confusion of motive : a chaos of the mind : a matter of muddled ethics. It is an integral part of Russian hospitality that they blackguard an ' ally ' to his face for the ' calumnious machinations ' practised by his Government in foreign affairs. The amusing thing about it is that this blackguarding is so deplorably inconsistent. One is apt to be shouted down for the ' betrayal ' of Kolchak, the ' annexation ' of the Caucasus, and the starvation by blockade by one's host, who will have it that all these diabolical acts have been deliberately designed by Mr. Lloyd George in order to ' humiliate ' Russia for her early exit from the war. But really all this angry denunciation is almost meant as a compliment : to show how much they like you personally despite your racial blackguardism, which they take for granted. Thus accosted, one is apt to become heated, stick up for the Government of one's country, and overstate facts. The room becomes a bear-garden.

Eisenstein opened the attack. ' Your allied diplomats,' he said, ' are hopeless. Some months ago I had occasion to see one of these worthy representatives of the diplomatic corps on behalf of a number of Jews that were in danger of being massacred by Kolchak's officers. The diplomat, my

client, by the way, was a marvellous linguist, a wonderful
specimen of humanity. There he sat before me, maintaining
a most distressing silence in twenty-eight foreign languages.
" I beg of you to intercede," I said, " to prevent their being
massacred. I entreat you, sir, to protest."

' " My dear Mr. Eisenstein," he said at last, " how can I
protest—before they are killed ? I want facts to go upon.
I cannot act before I have facts. Facts, Mr. Eisenstein,
facts ! "

' " Sir," I cried, " you will have *deadly* facts, if you are
satisfied to wait at all."

' " Anyhow," he said, " I am not going to risk my
reputation for flimsy rumours of this kind. I have been a
diplomatist now for thirty-six years, and never once in my
career, sir, have I said anything that—well, could be mis-
construed . . . to mean something. And I am certainly not
going to revise my methods now." And that was all I got
out of him.'

' You Allies,' said Uncle Kostia, ' have no sense of
humour. I'm a sedentary worker, a man of letters, no fighting man in any sense. I sit in my room all day and watch
your intervention through the window, so to speak. And
it amuses me to see how you are fussing over us and always
in the wrong direction, running about like clowns in a circus.
A naval gentleman of yours will arrive at the port, fresh
and raw from the high seas, and will be moved to request
enlightenment from his more experienced colleagues on this
rather elementary question : " Who is Kolchak ? Is he a
Bolshevik ? " He will be corrected in his erroneous supposi-
tion ; and then, a week later, he will begin to dabble in
Russian politics and will undertake brief excursions along
the coast and fire now and then, somewhat promiscuously,
at groups of villagers, whom in his simplicity he believes
to be Bolsheviks—boom—boom—boom—boom ! He will
set them flying in all directions, perhaps kill a cow or so.
After such a trip he will return to port, cheery and in good
spirits ; and after some little while the scattered villagers

will return to their village, consume the cow, and resume their interrupted occupations.—Wonderful minds you have! You will prop up some half-witted general and send in stores of clothing and munitions. And the fruit of it? The Bolshevik divisions wearing British uniforms with royal buttons, and the Bolshevik minority in Moscow nationally strengthened in the face of foreign enemies. I sit at my window, writing, reading, and the news dribbles through: " Omsk fallen. Kolchak shot. Allies packing up." It seems . . . silly.'

' Quite,' said the book-keeper Stanitski. It was a curious thing that the book-keeper Stanitski should not have been seen in Nikolai Vasilievich's household till the absence of finances in the firm of Nikolai Vasilievich provided him with nothing to record. Nikolai Vasilievich still went to his office ever afternoon to talk things over with Stanitski and possibly to keep up the feeling that he was still a business man ; and sometimes Zina would come and see him at his office. Stanitski was glad of these visits ; for he would then drop the paper he had been reading—there was absolutely nothing to do—and take part in their conversation. As business gradually dribbled down to nothing, one felt that the book-keeper Stanitski was becoming less of an employee and more of a friend and hanger-on. He was absolutely indispensable to Nikolai Vasilievich, for Stanitski was an optimist.

' Kolchak was impulsive and well-meaning,' said Eisenstein, ' but unfortunate in his selection of a task. He dismissed General Ditrich, who wanted to give up Omsk to save the Army, and replaced him by General Saharov, who undertook to keep Omsk ; whereon General Saharov lost both Omsk and the Army.'

' You Jews,' said the Admiral, ' are all damned Bolsheviks.' When the Admiral spoke of Jews he was filled with anger and, curiously, his face assumed a kind of Semitic expression.

' I wasn't, Admiral,' he said. ' I might be one now.

There may be a gleam of hope there at least. There's none here.'

' *I* wasn't one,' said Kniaz, his eyes and nostrils flaming with passion, ' till you Allies made me one ! ' The room grew still. We all turned round and stared at him. He had come in an hour or so ago, said nothing and consumed a box of chocolates all by himself. For twenty years or more he had said nothing. We felt that he had had ample time to think deep thoughts : and there at last he was pouring them out : giving us the benefit of all these years of silent contemplation : releasing the compressed fervour of his humiliated and down-trodden patriotism.

' Kniaz ! Kniaz ! ' cried Fanny Ivanovna in alarm. ' Kniaz ! '

But there was no stopping him. He spoke with the tremor and vehemence of a man who had held his tongue for twenty years. He overwhelmed us with surprise, but he seemed no less overwhelmed himself, flushed and marvelling at what was the matter with him. ' Why I personally object to your meddling in our affairs,' he cried, ' is because it implies the impression as if you could manage your own.' Fearful, flaming words spat from his fiery mouth. ' Ireland. India. Egypt.' Etc., etc., etc.

An Admiral contradicted by an adult person not subject to Naval regulations is a man at a disadvantage.

' They are just a pack of damned Bolsheviks, the lot of them, that's all they are,' said he.

' Jew-led, I suppose,' laughed Eisenstein.

' The Russian question,' said the Admiral, ' is a very big question, and I do not propose to discuss it here.'

' You have made it into a big question,' they all shouted, ' because you had not the imagination to foresee how it would grow into a big question when it was yet a little one.'

' I wonder,' said the Admiral, ' if you have held these views consistently throughout the revolution, if you had always been opposed to our help ? '

' Well,' said Kniaz, ' when I thought you would back up

a moderate democratic party I was at least more hopeful of the issue.'

' *Which* " moderate party," pray ? '

' Avksentiev's Government. The Directorate.'

' Oh, those ! ' scoffed the Admiral. ' They weren't much good. They did not believe in armies, and fighting, and that sort of thing.'

Kniaz looked up at him and pondered over the Admiral's uniform and probably thought that fighting, for the gallant sailor, was really an end in itself. And Kniaz concluded with the words : ' And now having thoroughly muddled up our issues, you leave us to the tender mercies of the Japanese.' But Sir Hugo, conceiving that they were arguing beside the point, snatched that phrase from him and stepped in between them with much dignity. He must have felt that the occasion called for a clear brain like his own to clear the misunderstanding.

' I think, Prince Borisov ' (and we all stared at Kniaz : it was indeed characteristic that Sir Hugo should be the first to know the Prince's name), ' that you are totally mistaken as to the object of the Allies in Siberia. You use that most unfortunate word " invasion." There was no question of " invasion." Our sole object in coming out to Russia, and the Admiral will confirm it, was to establish one indivisible national Russia by creating one strong united Russian Army—and that object, I am glad to say, we have now achieved.'

' One national Russia ! Excuse me, but—but—but—but if there is any national Russia to-day it is all on the other side. As for the Russian Army, the only Russian Army now is the Bolshevik Army. The others have all melted away.'

' Ho ! Kniaz is a Bolshevik ! ' cried Fanny Ivanovna.

' Ho ! ho ! ' cried the others.

' I will not argue about details, Prince Borisov. I am not a biologist and I don't dissect. And I don't propose to be dragged into pedantic microscopic analysis as to which is the particular political party to which the army, for the moment, swears allegiance. I am satisfied that it is a strong *Russian* Army, which it has been our object to create. And I will now say good-bye to you, and I will ask you to accept my very best wishes for the welfare of your great country, sir, and your personal welfare, too. Good-bye.'

The Admiral and Sir Hugo then vanished with Nikolai Vasilievich, and Fanny Ivanovna went after them into the little hall to see them out, while I remained behind.

' Sonia ! Vera ! Nina ! ' came from Fanny Ivanovna. ' How dark ! Light the *elektrichno* ! '

' Why don't you tell her,' I said to the three sisters, ' that it is not " *elektrichno*," but " *elektrichestvo* " ? '

' We've told her hundreds of times,' they replied in unison, ' but she will have it her own way " *elektrichno* " and " *elektrichno*." '

The Admiral's departure had set the ball spinning. Very soon the bulk of them was gone. And then the incredible happened. The three American boys arrived and took the three sisters to a dance. And on the eve of my departure ! I heard their laughing voices in the street, as the door closed upon them. That settled it. How they enjoyed themselves ! How they enjoyed life ! As for me, I would have to go home and pack.—That settled it.

I sat alone with Nikolai Vasilievich and Fanny Ivanovna.

' Wasn't Kniaz great ? ' said Nikolai Vasilievich.

' Who could have expected such eloquence from Kniaz ? ' said Fanny Ivanovna.

' Last night,' said Nikolai Vasilievich, ' Fanny Ivanovna and Kniaz sat alone and drank. They were quite drunk when I got home.' And he laughed in a sad, kindly manner.

' We only had a little port,' said Fanny Ivanovna. ' Kniaz drank but said nothing. He *is* a funny man. He bought some live chickens, and he keeps telling me every day at supper that he will bring me fresh eggs as soon as the chicks grow up and begin to lay. His contribution, you see, to the supper he consumes here ! The chickens have had time to grow into old hens—but the eggs are not forthcoming.

And when I say to him, " Kniaz, what about those eggs ? "
he answers in a tone as though I had wronged him, " But,
Fanny Ivanovna, they are only chickens yet." '

' He is always borrowing money from me,' said Nikolai
Vasilievich, ' and he owes me many hundred thousand
roubles—we have lost count, what with the exchange !—
and two days ago he borrowed forty roubles just to pay his
cab. He plays cards all day, and yesterday he won twenty
thousand roubles ; and when Fanny Ivanovna suggested
that he should pay me back, at any rate some of his debt, he
gave me back the forty roubles ! ' Nikolai Vasilievich smiled
again in a sad and kindly manner. What beautiful and kindly
eyes he had...

And then we talked of Petersburg and the old days, of
pre-war Easter, and their charming house in the Mohovaya.

' And do you remember the *Three Sisters*, Nikolai
Vasilievich ? '

' Don't I ! I was so wild that night because I had to miss
an appointment I had made with Zina. Oh, I was so wild
that night...' He looked at his watch.

' Well ! ' he said, and rose, yawning. ' I've got to go.'

He put on his coat, for the night was fresh and damp,
and his goloshes, as the roads were muddy. We heard the
door close on him as he went out.

' Always going to Zina's ? '

' Yes,' said Fanny Ivanovna. ' But it's quite all right.
They play cards there every night.' And then added for
further reassurance : ' He is passionately fond of cards—
and it keeps him occupied.'

' And do you remember that other play—at the Saburov? '

' Yes,' she said. ' Yes.—Oh, what was the ending of that
play ? We had to leave before the end. I was curious how
it would end. But I think you stayed to the last ? '

' Yes.—She is waiting for him to come back to her.
She is waiting confidently because he has left his silk hat on
the table. So she is waiting. But his valet comes and takes
the hat ; and she breaks down—and curtain ! '

' Oh,' she said.

' Nikolai Vasilievich liked it,' I observed.

' Did he like it ? '

She did not like it. By her face I could see that she did not like his liking it. It was as if the thing were peculiarly discordant with her own mood and trend of thought, as if she feared, against her hope, that Nikolai Vasilievich, in spite of all, might one day follow the example of the gentleman with the silk hat—and send Stanitski to her for his suits and underclothes.

She brooded.

' How long ago it seems,' she said at last. ' To think how long ago !—and we are still the same. Nothing has changed —nothing. Then it was the climax, and we held our breath expecting that now . . . now something *must* happen. Nothing happened. Then our whole life stood on edge, and the edge was sharp. We felt that the crisis could not last. We waited for an explosion. But it never came. The crisis still dragged on : it lapsed into a perpetual crisis ; but the edges blunted. And nothing happened. Life drags on : a series of compromises. And we drag along, and try to patch it up—but it won't. And it won't break. And nothing happens. Nothing ever happens. Nothing happens...'

' When I was very young,' I said, ' I thought that life must have a plot, like a novel. But life is most unlike a novel; more ludicrous than a novel. Perhaps it is a good thing that it is. I don't want to be a novel. I don't want to be a story or a plot. I want to live my life as a life, not as a story.'

' Yes,' she said, pursuing her own thought. ' Nothing happens. *Nothing*...'

The black night gazed through the window. The samovar produced melancholy notes. Tea was getting cold on the table.

## XII

' Would she come ? ' I thought, as next morning we drove off to the wharf. We passed a lonely square with a solitary Chink with a tin sword. That was the last we saw of Vladivostok.

The family came to see us off in practically its full strength. But she did not come. That settled it.

Nikolai Vasilievich was unshaven—a perfectly correct omission in a Russian gentleman. He wore blue spectacles, a bowler hat, a summer coat and goloshes. On the pier we talked of the political situation. The Admiral repeated but one phrase : ' We are not to blame.' The Russian General shook his head and blamed some vague, unknown power in rather vague, indefinite terms with a rather vague, indefinite blame, and then summed up the situation with ' I told you so ! ' though the substance of his telling was all very mysterious. But both fools and wise men alike had long given up the attempt to discover any meaning whatsoever in this resplendent General's utterances ; and if they listened to him at all, their attention was usually concentrated on his face or uniform or any other object near at hand.

She had not come. That settled it.

It rained, as on the day we arrived.

Then the Admiral came up to Nikolai Vasilievich to say good-bye. ' Well, Nikolai Vasilievich,' he said, ' what will you do ? '

' Well . . . I'll wait,' said Nikolai Vasilievich. ' I don't think it can be long now.'

PART IV

NINA

# I

AND this now is the ending, the *Liebestod* of my theme. We had left so suddenly. Her last words, look, gesture had 'settled it.' But now, in retrospect, the things that 'settled it' were, in their very vagueness, just the things striving to unsettle me, as I resumed my interrupted course at Oxford, having 'relinquished my commission,' thanks to the conclusion of the war. Was she *à moi*, or wasn't she? Well, was she? She was. She wasn't. Oh—how the hell could I know!

The art of living is the ability to subordinate minor motives to major ones. And it is an unsatisfactory art. You must make up your mind what you want, and when you have made up your mind what you want, you might as well, for the difference it makes to you, have never had a mind to make up. For the consequences have a way of getting out of hand and laying out the motives indiscriminately. And then *you* with your intent and will seem rather in the way. That is the truth.—(But it would serve us right if we thought so!)

Since childhood I had more or less earmarked my future, and the circumscription did not *really* take in Nina. I had in those early days conceived a novel that, oh! was to knock all existing novels flat. This novel was to be my goal in life, and then later on the novel was to follow my *real* life, a life of augmented splendour and achievement. Pending that achievement, there was, of course, that other life, essentially out of focus with the novel, not really life at all, a transitory, irritating phase not meriting attention. The novel was begun—invariably begun. The quite indefinably peculiar atmosphere of it seemed to defy the choice of language. For I happen to belong to that elusive class of people knowing several languages who, when challenged in one tongue, find it convenient to assure you that their knowledge is all in another. And I am one of those uncomfortable people whose national ' atmosphere ' had been somewhat knocked on the head—an Englishman brought up and schooled in Russia, and born there, incidentally, of British parents (with a mixed un-English name into the bargain!), and here I am. The war claimed me. And then, the war over, I looked at the novel. Heaven! How it had shrunk. I had contrived to overlook real life since it was out of focus with my novel, and now I found that it was just the novel that was out of focus with real life. Nothing more than that. But what a discovery! I had lived these years like an automaton, giving scarcely any heed to the life about me but vaguely cherishing the ' masterpiece,' and I found that I had really lived unconsciously and was alive, while the ' masterpiece ' had stifled and was dead.

It must have been at this point that the thought of Nina came to me identified with the idea of *living* as against *recording*. She would come to me in dreams. I was walking with some people, and she was walking with some other people. And then we met, and the people she was with stopped to talk to the people I was with, and she looked at me, a little bashful, ' repentance ' written on her face, as if to say, ' I am waiting '—but never said a word. And in my sleep the ' truth ' would dawn on me : ' So all this other . . . was mere whimsicality ? Oh yes, of course! I should have *understood* her.'

And in my waking hours, that were like dreams, involuntarily I would find myself asking General Bologoevski, whom I always went to see in town, if *he* ' understood her.' But the General understood nothing. ' I know why you are always coming here,' he once remarked. ' It is because I know her, because you want to talk to me of her... And you have reason to. My God! what eyes! What calves! What ankles! Look here : why in the world don't you marry her ? '

I had come to his hotel a while ago, which he had chosen on account of the ' nice little women there,' as he explained,

and overtook him in the act of making amorous advances
to the pretty chamber-maid who was giggling loudly in his
bedroom. ' English women,' he confided to me, ' always let
themselves go with foreigners. They're somehow ashamed
with their own countrymen. However.'
We went downstairs. ' Yes,' he sighed, ' things are
getting a little difficult just now. All I've got is ten pounds.
And when those are gone I won't know where to turn to.
And there's that motor-cycle I've bought, and they are
pressing me for payment. I give dem h-h-hell ! But it is all
a damrotten game, you know. The only consolation is that
it really is a good motor-cycle—a fine big thing. But there
seems no one I could borrow from.'
' But you *will* ride in taxis, General,' I gently reprimanded
him.
' Well, what is ten pounds ? ' he asked. ' Whether I ride
in taxis or go by bus, it's all one. It won't *last* in any case.
No : all my hope is in the claim I've lodged with the
Russian Embassy. I understand it's now only a question of
the Allies recognizing General Wrangel before the claim is
paid. But come, I'll introduce you to that Russian Colonel
there. He's been to Vladivostok and knows your friends,
no doubt—Nina. Come.'
We shook hands, and then compared experiences. ' And
do you remember that good-looking girl, Nina Bursànova ? '
at length I ventured.
The Colonel thought hard, and then said :
' No, I don't remember.'
Silence. The subdued hum of London was like the
burden note of a distant organ. Two other Russian Colonels
and a Captain, all of the Denikin Army, sauntered up, and
the General called the waiter and stood liqueurs and cigars
all round. The faint sounds of a hidden orchestra reached
our ears and set a match to the emotions stored away in my
sub-conscious warehouse... The tepid air within, sur-
rounded by the cold outside, the shaded lights contrasted by
the dark of night without, the easy atmosphere of crowded,

dazzling excitement, enshrouded by the loneliness of space, and our intimate seclusion within this gay tumultuousness —these things spoke. And the soft music told me that life *is*, and that she was all this that it meant...

No more novels! Life, I thought, was worth all the novels in the world. And life was Nina. And Nina was life. And, by contrast, the people I encountered seemed pretentious and insincere. The women in particular were unreal. They talked of things that did not interest them with an affected geniality. They pretended a silly superiority or else an unconvincing inferiority. They said ' *Really ?* ' and ' *Indeed ?* ' and ' How fascinating ! ' and ' How perfectly delightful ! ' Nina was not like that. My three sisters were not like that. They were real. They would laugh when they liked ; they would say exactly what they thought ; and they would say nothing if there was nothing to be said. Nina was so childish in her ways, and yet so very wise. She bit. She took water in her mouth and blew it out straight at your face, and threw herself on the sofa recklessly and stretched herself across, head downward.—She would never quite grow up. And by contrast, Oxford with its sham clubs and sham societies appeared a doll's house, a thing stationary and extinct of life, while the world, the Outside World, was going by. And I asked myself : What am I waiting for ?

In fine, it was Tristan pining for Isolde—with the important variation that Tristan journeyed to Isolde for the reason that Isolde failed to come to Tristan. One evening, very suddenly, I left England and set out back to the Far East.

## II

I travelled with Sir Hugo and the Russian General, and we took the eastern route. I had recognized Sir Hugo's gait as he came my way one day in crowded Piccadilly, but stopped in front of a shop window. And when I came up I saw Sir Hugo gazing at long rows of D.S.O.s and O.B.E.s

displayed behind the window. He was going out as pro-
fessional adviser—to Siam, I think, he said—or some such-
like place, and we arranged to leave together. And then the
General who was going out to Wrangel's Army in Constantinople joined us. He was to get off at Port Said.
On board next morning I showed the General an alarming
Reuter message from Constantinople. The French Government, it ran, had ordered the disbandment of General
Wrangel's Army, offering to transport the refugees back to
Russia or to Brazil, but General Wrangel declined the offer,
refused the invitation to go to Paris, and demanded the
return of his arms and munitions which the French had
already sold to Georgia, where they had fallen into Bolshevik
hands. Money, gold and silver valuables and jewels had
been stolen from the steamer in which General Wrangel was
staying. Important military documents regarding the cam-
paign in the Crimea had also been stolen.
  'I know,' he said, 'it is a most damrotten game, you
know. I give dem h-h-hell, those damrotten Frenchmen.
They are all damrotten Bolsheviks, they are.'
  'Well,' I said quietly, 'Kolchak has tried it. Denikin
has tried it. Yudenich has tried it. I should give it a rest
now.'
  'Ah,' he laughed, 'all this has merely been a little
rehearsal. We shall begin seriously in a year or two. It's the
only way to stop bloodshed.' He puffed at his heavy cigar
and his eyes twitched in the smoke.
  'A rehearsal.—Yes, I too intend to begin " seriously "
when I get to Vladivostok,' I laughed.
  'Is it not rather an adventure in futility?' Sir Hugo
asked.
  'He has taken my advice at last.' The General kissed his
finger-tips. 'What eyes !——'
  'What calves ! What ankles ! ' I completed automatically.
Silence.
  'The boat's beginning to roll.'
  'Where are all the passengers ? ' asked the General.

'I fear they must be indisposed,' Sir Hugo said, 'in consequence of the heavy sea.'

The General paused a little, gazing down at the cause of the passengers' indisposition. 'Of course,' he said, 'this rolling and pitching ought never to be.'

'Oh!' said Sir Hugo.

'It is entirely due to bad steering. Now on Russian ships when there is rolling or pitching the captain leaves his breakfast-table without a word, goes up to the man at the steering-wheel, beats him in the face the number of times he considers adequate (*v mordoo*, do you understand?)——'

Sir Hugo nodded to indicate that he understood.

'—and retires, without a word, to the saloon and continues his breakfast. And believe me, Sir Hugo, there is no more—ha, ha, ha—*rolling* or—ha, ha, ha—*pitching*! No more.'

'Hm,' said Sir Hugo. 'Doesn't the man at the steering-wheel ever . . . protest?'

'No,' said the General. 'He knows what it's for. The whole beauty of it is that the transaction is carried out swiftly, efficiently, quietly, without a sound—to everybody's satisfaction.'

'This quietude of method, General, seems to have produced, to put it mildly, quite a stir recently?'

'Not carried out quietly enough,' explained the General, indicating the root of the trouble.

'The times are dead and over, anyhow.'

'They are dead and over,' sighed the General, as if mourning a dear relation.

Silence again. The wind full of that vigour of the sea swept across my face.

'Do you see that ship there, sir?'

'*Which* ship *where*?' came the answer.

'*That* ship *there*,' said I, pointing at the only vessel on the only sea.

Sir Hugo looked.

'It's *not* a ship,' he said. 'It's a boat.'

'But, oh! sir,' I breathed in courteous remonstrance.

'Only His Majesty's ships are ships,' came the dry rejoinder. 'All other vessels are boats.—But to return to the question at issue, what were you going to say about the boat?'

'Well, I thought it was the *Aquitania*, but now I see it isn't,' I said, looking down into the green-blue waves. 'Do you remember the U-boat scare three years ago when we crossed to New York? It was a time when you felt that at any moment you might find yourself floating on the water owing to the disappearance of the boat.'

'The *ship*,' corrected Sir Hugo. 'The *Aquitania*—I mean the *boat*—I beg your pardon, you're right this time and I apologize. But why the devil didn't you say so straight out instead of wasting my time and your time with—with—with such a rubbishy matter?'

Ominous silence.

Then said the General, 'Perhaps we might go and have a drink?'

A week later we were entering the harbour of Port Said. We stood at the rail, balancing ourselves on our heels, as the liner, rolling heavily, turned into port.

'We're already four days late,' Sir Hugo said.

'I know. I have never been on such a damrotten ship before,' remarked the General. 'Now I remember on a Russian ship I once crossed the Pacific in, the captain promised to reach Yokohama by a certain date, but, as usual of course, failed to do so by a week or more. Well, all the passengers on board, officers and civilians, men and women, first-class passengers and even those who worked their passage, used to go up to the captain's cabin every morning and beat him in the face (*v mordoo*, you understand?) until it had swollen to, oh—oh——' (he indicated the size of the captain's face)—'immense proportions.'

'Hm,' said Sir Hugo, seemingly very interested. 'I think I caught you, General, saying " first-class passengers and

those who worked their passage." Now do you, or don't
you, purposely omit second-class passengers and such
passengers as may, or may not, have been going steerage ?
Or am I putting words into your mouth ? But let the matter
drift : it is of no consequence. My sympathies in this
incident, I hope you will forgive me, General, are all on the
side of the captain.'

The General listened, but did not understand. We parted
with him next morning, as we left Port Said.

Then, one afternoon, armed with binoculars, we peered
at the horizon to see if we could spot dry land. It was
towards seven in the evening that the throbbing liner came
into sight of Aden. She stole up carefully, and then lay still
outside the harbour.

We could feel the Sahara breathe upon us, like an oven.
I leaned across the rail and watched the sandy, ominous
desert coast, the strange, almost pathetic stillness of the
place, the malicious yellow water of the harbour.

I remember those disturbing, endless nights at Aden,
when I fancied that the boat would never move again. I
remember a kind of jeering look about that ancient liner
(captured from the Germans in the war) as she broke down
every now and then at God-forsaken places like Perim. I
was in a hurry, but circumstances had conspired to make
my journey inordinately slow.—But we were moving now
at last. I gazed at the sombre, yellow water as the liner
glided off the shark-infested coast of Aden in the heavy,
stifling silence of the eastern night. And it seemed to me that
from the surface to its depths the sea writhed in agony, and
that the sun-scorched desert withered in its age-long weari-
ness, all from a want of motive. And it seemed to me the
stars had spent themselves in waiting.

Then, one evening at Colombo, I parted with Sir Hugo,
who was changing boats for Singapore. We shook hands
warmly. ' Thank you so much for all your splendid,
excellent work,' he was saying ; and we were both obviously
touched. And though I did not know what the splendid,

excellent work he was thanking me for really was, I now
felt that it was enormous, overwhelming, but that I would
gladly do it all again, and more if necessary : so sweet was
it to be thanked! 'Splendid! Splendid!' he repeated, as
I helped him with his things. 'Good. Very good. Thank
you! Thank you again! Splendid! Splendid fellow!
Splendid fellow! Thank you! Good-bye!' And as he
settled in the throbbing motor-launch below, that then took
him ashore, he waved his hand to me and his lips seemed to
be moving still and saying 'Splendid!' Then he was gone
—on his new mission of advice.

I was sorry to part with the old man. There was a quality
about him that made him almost human. Later in the
journey I had a letter from him. '*We have had a good voyage,
so far,*' he wrote, '*with only two days' rough weather, when we
were skirting a typhoon, or a similar storm.*'

And now I was alone on board the old ocean liner, as
she steamed away carefully past the bright, foam-washed
breakwaters of Colombo's sunlit coast, and plunged into the
open sea.

I was in bed on deck, on the point of going to sleep.
Suddenly the dream of Nina, like a wave from nowhere,
flowed upon my brain. I was still awake that second : I
caught the dream as if with both my hands. I smiled broadly
to myself. I had *caught* a dream!

The sea was like a mirror of black glass. I listened to the
nocturnal silence. Now and then a wilful dolphin would
splash the surface of the water ; then everything was still.
The liner glided noiselessly across the sea.

Towards Singapore, Hongkong, Shanghai... I had
vague fears of being 'late.' In my emotional anxiety the
East itself appeared emotionally coloured. The eastern night
was veiled with sorrow. It was a night of *Why?* I discovered pathos in the animation of the Peking streets at
night. Even as I write I can see Canton with its narrow,
crowded streets sheltering beneath the dripping, over-

lapping roofs of shops, and feel the sombre enigmatic calm of their interior, the lethargic stare of Chinese merchants seated on the floor, and the thudding of the rain upon the roof ; and I can see the dull and yellow water of the rivers, the swarming multitudes of lives upon the quays, the *sampans* crowding the canals ; and I recall again the din of Mukden, the stretch of ancient muddy soil receding from my sight as I watched it from the window of the train, the fall of evening, and the melancholy of the ages. And I was made to feel that I was in another age, another world, that somewhere I must have dreamt this, or perhaps had known it ere I was born on earth, that deep in the recesses of my memory was an imprint of this peculiar light, this noise and din, this languid stillness of the East.

## III

Finally I arrived at Vladivostok. The moment I set my foot on the platform I flew by well-known streets and curves and turnings to their house. I remember I felt in the manner of Tristan at the end of the last act : very sure, impatient, overwhelmed with love. I felt that I would just fly into the room and cry ' *Isolde !* ' and she would fly into my arms— ' *Tristan !* ' And then, immediately, we would get busy with the love duet.

I knocked at the window, and I felt that they should hear the throbbing of my heart. I knocked again, and then the blind behind the window was tampered with, and there was Sonia peering at me through the glass. Her frown developed into a radiant smile and her voice rang through the building :

' Andrei Andreiech ! '

She ran away and then came to the door, half opened it, and said, ' Andrei Andreiech, we aren't dressed yet ; but come into the drawing-room—wait, let me run away first.'

It was about eleven o'clock in the morning. She ran away, and I went into the drawing-room. Everything was exactly as I had left it. The canary in the cage went on with his usual ' Chic ! . . . cherric ! . . . ' hopping to and fro. The sun was shining brightly through the window. It was one of those glorious autumn days that are like the unfolding days of spring.

' We shall be ready in ten minutes,' Sonia shouted from the adjoining room.

I waited ten minutes, and another ten minutes. Then the door opened and Sonia, radiant, came in. ' Nina will be ready in ten minutes,' she said.

' No, she won't be ready ! ' came Nina's voice—a discontented voice.

' Fanny Ivanovna and Kniaz have gone out shopping,' Sonia said.

' How is Nikolai Vasilievich ? ' I asked.

' He is probably at the office—or else with Zina.'

' How are the mines ? '

She only waved her hand.

' Hopeless ? '

' Oh, he *hopes*—we all *hope*, of course.'

' Well then,' said I, '. . . we must hope.'

Then Vera, radiant and marvellously pretty, came in. ' Nina will come in five minutes,' she said.

' Not in five but in ten minutes,' came Nina's voice, this time a whimsical voice.

I sat on the old sofa, and Sonia and Vera both stared at me in a curious manner, wondering, no doubt, why the dickens I had arrived.

Then the door of the adjoining room flew open, and Nina flitted in, shook hands without looking at me and flitted over to the window.

I still sat on the old sofa, of which the spring had burst, and no one spoke. It was a somewhat silly situation.

' That spring I am sitting on is burst,' I said at length.

' Oh, Vera burst it,' Nina said.

' It's a lie ! ' Vera flared. ' You know yourself you burst it last night when you jumped about with Ward.'

' No, it's Vera,' Nina said.

' It's a lie ! a lie ! a lie ! '

' It really doesn't matter in the least who burst it,' I intervened. ' I noticed that the spring was burst because I happened to be sitting on it . . . otherwise everything seems to be very much the same.'

We sat still for a little while. Then Nina turned to me impulsively and said, ' And you haven't seen the three sisters ! '

I stared at her with blank expression.

She ran out, and returning quickly, thrust three tiny kittens on my lap. The old cat followed her into the room and looked up at me suspiciously.

' This is Sonia. This is Nina. This is Vera,' she explained.

For a while we admired the ' three sisters ' ; then with the same swift motion, she grabbed the kittens in her hands and carried them away. The old cat followed her back into the adjoining room.

Again there was silence. The canary in the cage went on : ' Chic ! . . . cherric ! . . .'

' And Andrei Andreiech always goes on with his Chic ! . . . cherric ! . . .' said Nina.

' Which Andrei Andreiech ? '

She pointed at the canary.

' What do you mean ? '

' We call him Andrei Andreiech.'

' Why ? '

' Oh, just so—there is something of you about him— something—unsubstantial.'

' Nina, come for a walk,' I said.

I helped her on with her coat.

We went by the Aleutskaya, bathed in sunshine, switched off down the Svetlanskaya and turned into a park overhanging the sea. Autumn stood at the door with its sombre moods of hopes frustrated, of joys gone, and aims blown to the wind, like leaves of autumn.

'Why did you come?' she said. 'Why? I never asked you.'

'You told me that you love me,' I said.

'I never loved you.'

'Why did you lie then?' I cried.

'Go to the devil!' she answered, and turned her face away.

'I have been three months on the way . . . three months. Good God, Nina, travelling *three months* to come and see you—and there!'

'It was an unusually long journey. You must have been moving very slowly.'

'There!' I went on protestingly, 'I chuck Oxford, come all the way to Vladivostok, spend three months on the journey—because—because I love you, and you——'

'You have a speck of soot on your nose,' she remarked.

'Nina!' I cried laughing, my heart all weeping tears. 'Nina!'

'Go and wash your face,' she said, 'and then come back again. I'll wait for you here.'

I gave it up. We sat together, saying nothing, and something about the autumn sun, the wind that came defiant from the roaring sea and harassed the fallen yellow leaves at our feet, suggested that I was late in the season with my love—perhaps too late. *Tristan* became a thing alien and remote, and I felt that I was singing in an altogether different opera.

IV

We did not go home. She said, 'I'm tired of seeing Papa, Fanny Ivanovna and Kniaz. They always quarrel, always quarrel... Kniaz is the best of the lot.' Instead we went to the Olenins who lived in a remote *datcha* by the sea. It was a place scarcely accessible by night, for there was not a light and the roads were pools of mud. The environment concentrated all the angry dogs and robbers in the town.

We found Sonia and Vera there chatting with the three American boys, now known as the 'three brothers.' The hostess seated at the piano was sending forth sounds of syncopated music, and then the three sisters with their corresponding 'brothers' danced, while I was left alone with my sense of the three months' journey east gnawing at my heart.—The fact of the matter was that I failed to see exactly where *I* came in in this combination.

I strolled into the dining-room with its familiar pictures in gilt frames, poorly furnished. Colonel Olenin, now out of work, was playing cards with a brother officer, also out of work, and with Zina's father, while a Japanese paying guest was looking on, picking his teeth the while. Madame Olenin, little Fanny clinging to her skirt, came up and stood, a little bored, and with that look of hers as though she could have loved a lot.

'You do not dance?' the paying guest inquired on our being introduced. 'Why?'

'Andrei Andreiech is smitten,' said Madame Olenin.

'Ah!—Iz zas so—zzz——?'

'Has lost his heart to Nina.'

The paying guest chuckled and picked his teeth. 'Ah!— Iz zas so?' he said and sucked his breath in '—zzz--' as Japanese do in their politeness. 'Ah!—Very nice! Very nice!'

'Andrei Andreiech wants to marry her,' continued Madame Olenin.

'Ah!—Iz zas so?—zzz—Very nice! Very nice!'

'But she doesn't want to,' I said.

'Ask her,' she said.

'I have asked her. She won't.'

'Well, you ask her again.'

'How many times?'

'Never mind how many times. Go on asking her. If you go on at it long enough any woman will give way. You go on asking her. Or else marry our little Olya, our little football. You'll suit each other well.'

The paying guest chuckled loudly and picked his teeth.
She was trifling, trifling with a serious question, and I
smiled, as one smiles on these occasions—an economic and
reluctant smile.

I learnt that one of the veteran grandfathers had died a
month ago ; the other was alive. He sat and frowned before
him, and little Fanny seemed to shun his frown each time
she passed him in the dining-room. I spoke to him and
found that he would not admit that any revolution had ever
taken place in Russia. ' Nonsense,' he kept saying. ' Nonsense. In France there has been a revolution. But this is
Russia. This is not France.'

' But—but what of the Bolsheviks ? ' I asked.

The antiquated veteran suddenly relapsed into a fit of
anger. ' I'll show these Bolsheviks ! ' he threatened. ' I'll
make them dance ! I'll stand no nonsense ! Not I ! They'll
soon see the man they've got to deal with ! They'll get short
shrift from me, I can tell you ! I'll show these Bolsheviks !
I'll make them sing ! ' The feeble old man was seized by a
violent fit of coughing. His body shook and reeled, and his
vain threats only emphasized the wretched impotence, the
piteous weakness of his senility. Madame Olenin came to
his rescue and beat him on the back to alleviate his coughing
and prayed him not to talk of the wicked Bolsheviks as it was
injurious to his health, but even through his coughing,
choking hopelessly, he threatened angrily : ' I'll show these
Bolsheviks ! I'll make them sing !—these Bolsheviks ! I'll
make them dance ! ' and then again relapsed into a violent
fit of senile coughing.

Uncle Kostia, as I went to him, was sitting on the sofa,
unshaven and unkempt, in the dim and dreary light of early
evening. An empty glass of tea stood on the table. ' They
are dancing,' he said, with a strange gleam in his eye. ' Let
them dance. They think I am useless. Let them think.
They've been complaining of me ? '

' Who, Nikolai Vasilievich ? '

' No, he wouldn't, I respect him. The *others*. I know

they have. It's life's own joke that its superior humanity is not good enough for their inferiors. To the superior humanity the provocation is past a joke, I can tell you ; to the inferior, the situation is just a matter of fact ; so whose is the joke unless it is life's own ? Life is like that. Here am I—writing away unselfishly. Heaven only knows if what I write will be published in my lifetime. Then, years afterwards, they will read my books ; they will think of me, wonder how I looked and spoke and felt. And I won't know...'

' Yes. But to dwell prematurely on the sadness of one's death to others, Uncle Kostia, is like asking for money in advance. It's commercially unsound.'

Then, as our talk continued, I became aware of awful symptoms of Uncle Kostia's condition. Uncle Kostia assured me positively that he had never had a father : that he was the son of his grandfather. And when I pointed out that the omission seemed to me to err a little on the side of the extravagant, he replied quite earnestly that he did not ' see it.'

## V

Such pitiful, heartrending scenes as this became a frequent occurrence. Each of the three sisters walked arm in arm with each of the ' three brothers,' and I trailed alone behind them, a kind of tutor, with a heinous sense of my three months' voyage ripening into a grievance. A poor thing, sir, but mine own ! The three sisters, escorted safely home, would cry out from the house steps, ' Good night, Brothers ! ' The ' three brothers ' then would answer, ' Good night, Sisters ! ' I alone said nothing. I felt that an additional ' brother ' might spoil the symmetry of the arrangement. The fact of the matter, as you will see, was that I was not one of the ' three brothers.' That settled it.

A very similar situation would ensue at dances, those delightful dances of the American Red Cross. We, that is,

the three sisters, the 'three brothers' and I (the odd number), would drive down in an American Service limousine,
rolling gently through the dark and gruesome streets, the
mellow moon shining feebly on the muddy road. Next we
entered that long draughty room in the Naval Barracks
taken over by the American Red Cross. In a little while the
three sisters reappeared in the room, looking the bouquet
that they were, that big nigger band would blurt out its
syncopated music, and they would slide away in the embrace
of the 'three brothers' and vanish in a paraphernalia of
Allied uniforms, while I was reduced to being a 'wall-
flower,' or else to dance with plump and heavy women,
which after my experience with Nina felt very much like
moving heavy chairs about the floor. It was idiotic to
have travelled sixteen thousand miles to do this sort of thing!
—That settled it.

I dare say it was my fault—but my somewhat inartistic
intrusions on a party that was otherwise complete, began to
tire Nina. She asked me to give up 'pursuing' her. I
resolved not to pursue her. I told her so. I kept telling her
so. My passionate explanations of my aloofness began to
anger her. My vehement assurances of resignation to my
lonely lot struck her as discordant and dishonest. And she
conferred on me the sentence which in love is hardest of all
sentences to bear—the sentence of indifference. Now there
is but one way to combat indifference in love, and that is by
a feud. You tell yourself: She may think of the quarrel
at times, perhaps regret the loss, or be annoyed, or feel
hostile. There is then some link between you and her.
However small, that is at least something. Indifference is
simply nowhere. Acting on these lines, my three months'
journey always in my mind, I developed a grievance that
outraged my soul. I swore there and then to myself that
never again, so long as I lived, would I go to see Nina. That
settled it.

I found myself going there that same afternoon, it seemed
in spite of myself and partly under the influence of the wine

that I had consumed at lunch. The day was a peculiarly
sunny and friendly kind of day and the blue sky and the clear
air and even the shops themselves seemed to beckon to me
not to be a fool, not to stand upon my silly dignity ; and so
I discovered, as I walked along till I could see their house
beckoning to me in the distance, that her indifference, even
if confirmed (and I now refused to confirm it), had the overlooked advantage of admitting me of being in her presence.
But when I returned I found I had innumerable occasions
to revert to my original interpretation of indifference.

And feeling that my affairs were in a bad way I made a
bold *coup* to regain my tottering prestige. I appeared furiously, almost indecently intellectual, talked in quick
succession of Turgenev, Goethe, Dostoevski, Chehov,
Flaubert, Shakespeare and Tolstoy. It impressed nobody.
She hardly listened to me. So I tried Wagner, Scriabin,
Debussy and Richard Strauss. Nothing doing. I tackled
Ibsen, Schopenhauer, Nietzsche, Shaw, Bennett, Chesterton
and H. G. Wells ; quoted them. It cut no ice. She showed
that this sort of thing ' did not go down with her ' at all.
Clearly she wasn't ' having any.' And the great men, I fear,
looked small beneath her scornful look.

I met her once in the street. It had been snowing in the
night, prematurely for the season ; now the snow was
thawing and the ground was muddy. The sun was yellow,
honey-coloured, and her side-long look seemed warmer in
the sunshine.

' Will you marry me ? ' I said.

' No.' She shook her head. ' I am tired of you.'

' I know that,' I replied, and walked silently beside
her.

' If I were really tired of you I wouldn't tell you.'

' Then why do you tell me ? ' I took it up, hungering for
something positive, however small.

' I don't always say what I think,' was the answer.

We walked on.

' We are leaving in any case,' she said.

' When ?  Where ? '

' Next month—for Shanghai. Mama is going to start a business there. Hats. We have to do *something*.—We shall have a good time in Shanghai.'

' Ah, you won't ! ' I said.

She looked at me.

' What of your " three brothers " ? ' I gloated.

' Their ship is going there next month. Aha ! Do you think Mama would get us to come otherwise ? '

' Good riddance ! ' I said.

' What's happened ? '

' Go ! ' I cried. ' But for heaven's sake *go*. Off with you ! I haven't time to waste. I want to get back. I am missing my examination ! '

' You can go back now if you like. I'm not keeping you.'

' What's the matter with you ? '

' What's the matter with *you* ? '

' I shall see you off first,' I said, ' and then I'll go.'


# VI

And then I only wished that they would go, and that I could return at once to England. The date of sailing was put off from week to week because of passport difficulties and dearth of accommodation in the steamers of the Russian Volunteer Fleet. I was frightened lest they should not be able to get away. For if they stayed, my soul was ruined.

And then, thank heaven, they were going.

Fanny Ivanovna and Nikolai Vasilievich preferred to part with them in their own rooms. It was, I think, because they would rather hide their emotion from the people who they knew were sure to come to see the girls off on the boat, and also, I think, because the relations with Magda Nikolaevna were not entirely satisfactory.

Yesterday I had met them in the Aleutskaya as they

returned from the restaurant 'Zolotoy Rog,' where they
now always went to lunch : the cooking arrangements in
the rooms were thoroughly inadequate. Nikolai Vasilievich
in his mackintosh and bowler hat looked markedly older
and more worn than he had looked two years ago. Perhaps
it was the shrewd light of the afternoon that scrutinized his
features. There was a curious, mysterious, Mona Lisa look
about the face of Fanny Ivanovna : as if she knew a thing
or two : as if she had grounds for reassurance. And had
she not ? The partnership with Magda Nikolaevna was an
engaging proposition. The only two deterrents to her going
into partnership with Magda Nikolaevna were those two
unfortunate words that had not lost their sting for her—
' governess ' and ' lapdog.' She told me she might overlook
the ' governess ' : the suggestion had not a shadow of
foundation and could be forgiven—at a pinch. But the
' lapdog '—never ! Henceforth, as in the past, their destiny
hung on the mines, and Fanny Ivanovna's ideas as to their
recovery were somewhat mixed. But the Japanese were now
in possession of the Province, and if Nikolai Vasilievich got
back his mines she said she would be able to return to Germany. She hated Vladivostok. And yet, she told me
privately this morning, they had been so long together, had
gone through so much misery together, that she doubted if
she could ever leave him. And even if the mines materialized,
she thought—there was that suspicion in her heart and
consequently that look of reassurance in her face, that
youthful ease about her manner—that the passion between
Nikolai and Zina was wearing off. And—nothing ever
happens...

They were both visibly perturbed. Nikolai Vasilievich
walked up and down the room, obviously to hide his
emotion. The luggage had already been removed to the
boat, and the three sisters, dressed for the voyage, had sat
down before the final parting. Kniaz read his paper to himself, and we talked inconsequently of anything and everything, and incidentally I learnt that Uncle Kostia, in

pursuance of a logical analysis of his position as an author, had arrived at the conclusion that it was futility to get up at all, and of late conformed to his discovery.

' *And*——' said I significantly.

' Yes—yes,' said Nikolai Vasilievich knowingly. ' I'm sorry for him.'

Fanny Ivanovna surveyed the three sisters with a doleful look. ' *Ach*, Nikolai Vasilievich ! ' she said. ' Look at us ! Even our children are leaving us. There will be no one left when they are gone but you and I and Kniaz and the kittens. Sonia, Nina and Vera, the kittens. The real Sonia, Nina and Vera have lost patience with us.'

' Don't, Fanny Ivanovna, don't,' Vera murmured.

' And we have lived together a long time, through a maze of trouble, yet I think we lived happily—as happily as we could. Why that parting now ? Why ? '

Someone sighed, and Nikolai Vasilievich turned his face away.

' Now it is October. It will soon be winter and this roof and yard will be deep in snow. Outside it will be cold and dark and wretched, and we shall be short of wood, and there will be another *coup d'état*. But you and I, Nikolai Vasilievich, you and I will be here—going out to lunch at the " Zolotoy Rog " then as ever—ever ! '

She sighed deeply. ' What shall we do all by ourselves in the winter?'

Nikolai Vasilievich, his hands deep in his trouser pockets, stood at the window and did not answer. When he was perturbed, I noticed, he always stood at the window with his hands deep in his trouser pockets, and thought. And I fancied that he must be thinking : Strange were the ways of the world : there ! all along he had planned to escape from her—but life has taken its course, and nothing has come of it. And now those others, for whom he had stayed, were going away from him, and he, the would-be deserter, was left all alone with her ; and in a thousand and one indefinable ways she has captured him. And when I met his eyes

I had a feeling, an unmistakable feeling, that indeed I was right in my surmise.

Then came that hush, familiar in farewells, that comes in anticipation of the signal. Nikolai Vasilievich pulled out his watch and said, ' Well——'

We rose, and I went out and waited for them in the street. Then they came out. Fanny Ivanovna, Nikolai Vasilievich and Kniaz stood on the steps and looked at us, as we walked away, turning round again and again as we went. The sharp autumn wind ruffled Nikolai Vasilievich's scanty hair, and the three of them, as they stood there hatless in the open, looked frail and weak and helplessly exposed to the storms of life. Then Kniaz went back into the house, as if in a hurry to resume an interrupted occupation. We looked round a last time, and turned the corner. The three sisters blew their noses frequently and gulped, and Vera's eyes were red. And as I went I too was thinking : Strange were the ways of the world : there ! I had arrived from the other end of the earth in time to see them off on a two-days' trip : to assist at an ordinary farewell in this unholy outskirt of the world, when I ought to be swotting hard for my Final Schools ! And, by contrast, Oxford seemed a place of *doing things*.

Even now that they have gone and the steamer is about to reach the docks of that far eastern Paris, I can see them very vividly before me as they stood on the deck of the *Simbirsk* : three pretty kittens, each lovelier than the other and quite irresistible together. It was long over two hours since we had been told to clear the decks, but the steamer was still there. I stood on the quay with Magda Nikolaevna, who was to follow her three daughters in a day or two by rail, and while she was telling me delightful tales of Nina's childhood, I looked at Nina leaning with her folded hands upon the rail and her chin upon her folded hands, looking at us with that exquisite, disquieting side-long look, evidently intent on catching what her mother was telling me about her. I do not remember how long I stood there. There were the ' three brothers ' to see them off, on the eve of their own departure for Shanghai ; then they left : they had to get back to their ship. Time after time I would go up close to the steamer ; but I gathered from her look that the effort was superfluous : there was nothing we could talk about. Each time I went back and stood by Magda Nikolaevna and the Olenins and wished to heaven that the steamer would depart. But the steamer, despite all its hooting, seemed intent on remaining. Then, suddenly, I understood that it was indeed impossible to keep on standing there for ever. I felt that this was now the end and that now I must make haste to go. I turned to Magda Nikolaevna and the Olenins, and we shook hands ; then I approached the boat and waved good-bye to them. Nina stretched her hand down to me without a word ; but a handshake would have involved a cold bath !

I went hastily, without looking back. I walked briskly to the ' Zolotoy Rog ' and lunched lavishly and drank much wine—a luxury in these times !—as if to celebrate the occasion of my soul's release. I felt as if I was being freed from prison. I sat in the crowded, heated restaurant and watched the life bubbling about me—watched it in excitement, in exultation. But after lunch I thought I wanted to make certain—for real freedom could not come till I was certain—that the steamer had finally departed. Accordingly I strolled down to the wharf of the Volunteer Fleet. As I approached it I perceived the two impassive funnels of the *Simbirsk* still showing from above the godowns. I turned back into town, my mind a rising sea of tribulation. I longed to see the end of it, to know that they had gone. Why this heartrending delay ? I paced the streets of Vladivostok, seething with emotion. I must have looked odd that afternoon, for strangers turned round in the streets to look at me as I passed. I walked on and on, increasing my pace as I did so. An hour later, or thereabouts, I made my way back to the wharf. The steamer was still there. I turned back into town. I could scarcely endure the torture of the suspense. I walked the length of the Svetlanskaya, and then switched off until I reached the race-course. I turned into the wood. I climbed the hills.

Then, late in the afternoon, before twilight had set in, I made my way back to the wharf. My heart sick with palpitation, I looked over the godowns of the Volunteer Fleet. The steamer had departed. I went past innumerable barrels piled together, steam-heating pipes and wire rusting in the open, machinery dumped on the quay, and bales of cotton rotting in the dockyard, until finally I stood on the very spot where I had parted with them. The space at the quay where the *Simbirsk* had been showed empty ; dull, dirty water heaved at my feet and a cork from a bottle and some bits of wood heaved upon it. I looked out upon the sea for a sign of the steamer. It had completely vanished. I peered at the horizon to see if I could spot the smoke from its two funnels. But there was none.

William Gerhardie was born in St Petersburg in 1895 and was educated there and at Oxford. In the First World War he served in the Royal Scots Greys, was attached to the British Embassy in Petrograd and joined a British Military Mission to Siberia in 1920 for which he was awarded the OBE. His first novel *Futility* was published in 1922. His other works include *The Polyglots, Of Mortal Love, God's Fifth Column* and *Memoirs of a Polyglot*. He died in 1977.

# THE WORKS OF WILLIAM GERHARDI

1. *Futility* : a novel on Russian themes, depicting a father gathering dependants as his hopes rise and his fortunes sink through four succeeding stages of the Russian social scene ; the narrator, an Englishman of Russian upbringing, revealing, against this humorously and geographically changing but tragically unchanging background, the pathos of his growing love for the second of three bewitching daughters.  1922.

2. *Anton Chehov* : a critical and biographical study.  1923.

3. *The Polyglots* : a novel developed whilst he lives his narrative by a highspirited young man who, in the course of travelling on a military mission to the Far East, discovers his relatives, their children and friends—a multitude of comic characters impelling themselves into his novel, narrowing down his own activities to the seduction of an adorably inconsequent cousin married off against her will, his purer nature dedicated to a tender friendship with a child of nine, promising to grow up into an exquisite young girl, the spiritual answer to his yearning being, it may be—he sees it half foreshadowed across the years —his one true love, only to die suddenly, inexplicably, on board the homing liner and to be buried at sea.  1925.

4. *A Bad End* : ' an étude on the black notes ' about an unintentional act of manslaughter, the trial for murder, conviction and execution of Mr. Proudfoot ;· declared as unlikely by most of the critics, but confirmed by a former Lord Chancellor (Lord Birkenhead) in given circumstances as certain.  1926.

5. *Donna Quixote* : a play, of which the first act is a farce, the second a comedy, and the third a tragedy ; about a woman who, though her youth was tarnished by one lapse (the consequence, a literary critic, making his appearance in the play), goes through life taking care of other people's morals, until, as she lies dying, it dawns on her that she has been living other people's lives instead of her own.  1927.

6. *The Vanity-Bag :* a study in literary compression, containing in sixty pages all the elements of a novel ; about a middle-aged American who falls in love with a girl in Salzburg, whose vanity-bag must needs convince him in the end that he has nothing more to hope from her, and is rewarded by the unsought heavy friendship of her literary father—a bag of vanity. 1927.

7. *Pretty Creatures :* containing the two short novels, as well as one long-short story, *Tristan und Isolde*, and two short stories, *The Big Drum*, and *In the Wood.* 1927.

8. *My Sinful Earth :* a novel of the Twenties, foreshadowing the coming of our era, culminating in the atomic disintegration of all but a handful of refugees in an hotel on a rounded mountaintop isolated from the earth and now circling the sun—a token world for the vanished planet. 1928.

9. *Pending Heaven :* a novel about two men treading the donkeyround of paradise deferred, their literary friendship strained to breaking-point by rivalry in love : ending in marriage as a resting-place for the one ; for the other, in resignation, illness and an inspired vision, seen in delirium, of the indestructible essences streaming forth from the broken images of life, followed by his discovery that death has done no more than stop his reading in the book of life a sorry page, confused and deceptive and couched in metaphor and rhetoric, whereas now he could go where he liked, be what he liked. 1930.

10. *Memoirs of a Polyglot :* an autobiography transmuting extraordinary experiences into ordinary experiences by the process of recording that which has been actually felt, not what one feels he was expected to feel ; about his parents and grandparents, his own childhood in St. Petersburg, where his father, a British cotton manufacturer, settled in the Nineties, his Russian school days, his joining the Scots Greys in the First World War, the cavalry cadet squadron in Ireland, his commission and transfer to the British Embassy at Petrograd, where he saw the Russian Revolution in all its stages, and his service on the British Military Mission to Siberia, followed by his going up to Oxford,

and afterwards living in many countries, making life his vocation and distilling it in fiction. 1931.

11. *The Memoirs of Satan :* a history of mankind presented through the imaginary experiences of Satan who, at crucial moments in the lives of famous figures, real and legendary, enters them in turn to enable him to give the inside story in every case. In collaboration with Brian Lunn. 1932.

12. *The Casanova Fable :* with Hugh Kingsmill ('The Summing-Up'). 1934.

13. *Resurrection :* an autobiographical novel recording a true experience out of the body, followed that night by a London ball at which, against a background of social comedy, the theme is taken up and developed into a passionate argument for the immortality of the soul, illustrated by the spontaneous recollection of a year rich in travel and having the power to evoke a vanished lifetime in a day : the day of the occult experience which, incredible though it may seem, is not unique. 1934.

14. *Meet Yourself* (as you really are) : about three million detailed character studies through self-analysis. In collaboration with Prince Leopold Loewenstein-Wertheim. 1936.

15. *Of Mortal Love :* a novel containing fresh love-lore and treating of the succeeding stages of transmutation of love erotic into love imaginative ; of love entrancing into love unselfish ; of love tender into love transfigured : being one of those 'stories of a simple heart' which is the novelist's supreme ambition and delight but is put off from year to year for work less tender and more easy of accomplishment—an intention, needing the mellow touch, the author was urged by Katherine Mansfield in 1922 not to abandon. 1936.

16. *My Wife's the Least of It :* a novel unfolding a humorous tragedy against a background of social comedy ; being the inside history of the peregrinations and vicissitudes of a film script and of Mr. Baldridge, its unfortunate author, his fall, incarceration, renaissance, marriage and rise to a position of unprecedented public esteem in the administration of charities. 1938.

17. *The Romanovs :* an historical biography of the dynasty written as a narrative rather than as a compilation, the earlier dynasty of the Ruriks being also included, thus providing a survey of over a thousand years, not merely of Russian rulers, but of their opposite numbers in Europe : an evocation of the past as a mirror for the present—substantially a history of Russia. 1940.

" What They Said at the Time ": see Introduction to the Collected Edition, in *Futility*, page xix.